'At once familiar and t̲   e
pleasure to see his work translated at last in these beautifully
produced English editions'   *Sunday Times*

'Will appeal to fans of Agatha Christie looking for a new case to
break'   *Irish Times*

'A stellar whodunit set in 1940s Japan… The solution is a perfect
match for the baffling puzzle. Fair-play fans will hope for more
translations of this master storyteller'
Publishers Weekly, Starred Review

'With a reputation in Japan to rival Agatha Christie's, the master of
ingenious plotting is finally on the case for anglophone readers'
Guardian

'A delightfully entertaining locked room murder mystery… An
ideal book to curl up with on a winter's night'   *NB Magazine*

'Never anything less than fun from beginning to end… Truly
engrossing'   *Books and Bao*

'A classic murder mystery… Comparisons with Holmes are justi-
fied, both in the character of Kindaichi and Yokomizo's approach
to storytelling—mixing clues, red herrings and fascinating social
insight before drawing back the curtain to reveal the truth'
Japan Times

'The perfect gift for any fan of classic crime fiction or locked
room mysteries'   *Mrs Peabody Investigates*

MURDER
AT THE
BLACK CAT CAFE

&

WHY DID THE
WELL WHEEL CREAK?

SEISHI YOKOMIZO

**Translated from the Japanese
by Bryan Karetnyk**

Pushkin Press
Somerset House, Strand
London WC2R 1LA

First published in Japan in 1973 as
KURONEKOTEI JIKEN / KURUMAIDO WA NAZE KISHIRU
(in "HONJIN SATSUJIN JIKEN") by KADOKAWA CORPORATION, Tokyo.

English translation rights arranged with KADOKAWA CORPORATION,
Tokyo through JAPAN UNI AGENCY, INC., Tokyo.

First published by Pushkin Press in 2025

ISBN 13: 978-1-80533-551-1

A CIP catalogue record for this title is available from the British Library

The authorised representative in the EEA is eucomply OÜ, Pärnu mnt. 139b-14,
11317, Tallinn, Estonia, hello@eucompliancepartner.com, +33757690241

Designed and typeset by Tetragon, London
Printed and bound in the United Kingdom by Clays Ltd, Elcograf S.p.A.

Pushkin Press is committed to a sustainable future for our
business, our readers and our planet. This book is made from
paper from forests that support responsible forestry.

MIX
Paper | Supporting
responsible forestry
FSC
www.fsc.org
FSC® C018072

www.pushkinpress.com

3 5 7 9 8 6 4

CONTENTS

MURDER
AT THE
BLACK CAT CAFE

PROLOGUE

My dear Mr Y——,

Please forgive my long silence. When last you wrote, you mentioned that you were ill, but, judging from the fact that the publication of *Death on Gokumon Island* carries on apace, I trust that it was nothing too serious. I read the monthly magazine instalments with avid interest. While there are one or two parts that seem to me a little exaggerated, I realize this cannot be helped when it comes to novel-writing. I do hope you will continue to write them. (Only, please, be gentle with me!)

Now, then. When I last paid you a visit, you said to me something along the following lines. That with *The Honjin Murders* you were able to write a kind of 'locked room' mystery, and now you would like to try your hand at a 'faceless corpse' one; and that if I were ever to come across such a case, you would be grateful if I would provide you with the materials. Well, my friend, and what do you suppose my very first case was after I arrived in Tokyo? Why, yes! The 'faceless corpse' mystery that you were hoping for. And what's more, it was quite different from the so-called 'faceless corpse' formula that you described to me.

Ah, my dear Y——! I cannot help recalling that fusty old saying: that truth is stranger than fiction. At the outset of *The Honjin Murders*, you wrote that we ought to be grateful to the murderer for having hatched that ingenious plan. Very well! Now you shall have to sing the praises of the villain who planned this horrific 'faceless corpse' case. It may not have the elegance or beauty of *The Honjin Murders* or the triple murder in *Death on Gokumon Island*—in which regard you may be somewhat disappointed—and yet, in terms of the sheer blackness and bestial savagery of the killer's plan, it is altogether in a league of its own. At least, that is my opinion; for now, though, I shall refrain from saying too much more about it. I have posted to you separately all the relevant documents and leave the rest to your good judgement. The documents are numbered sequentially, so please read them in that order. I am eager to see how you will digest the material and adapt these miscellaneous records.

Respectfully yours…

It was the spring of 1947 when this letter from Kosuke Kindaichi reached me in that little village in the Okayama countryside where I had been evacuated during the war.

Imagine my excitement as I read the letter! But then, was it truly excitement that I felt? Or was it not a sense of dread? The detective's words had made such a strong impression on me, and I could tell that this was no ordinary case. But still, this was the 'faceless corpse' mystery for which I had so longed!

The documents that had been sent separately arrived three days after the letter. What follows is an account based on those documents, a record of that heinous crime and the deductions that exposed it. But before I get to that, I had better clarify my relationship with Kosuke Kindaichi.

It all came about in the late autumn of the previous year, when, in the rural village where I had been evacuated, I received an unexpected visitor.

I was poorly at the time, and all I seemed to do was sleep. On the date in question, I had spent the entire day dozing as I lay sprawled out on the futon. The others in the house had gone off to dig for yams in the fields on the mountainside, leaving me all alone. But just then, a man came clattering in.

Given that the building was a farmhouse, there were none of those smart features—a vestibule, for instance— that I had in my own home. Instead, the front door opened onto a broad earthen-floored room with an imposing shoji

11

screen on the other side. This shoji was awfully heavy and difficult to open and close, so it would be left ajar throughout the day. On the other side of the earthen floor there was a tatami room about twelve square feet in size, and beyond it a slightly larger sitting room, visible from the entrance through the open *fusuma*. It was there that I would always sleep. Because of a longstanding chest condition, I was used to keeping doors and windows open, and so, whenever I had the opportunity, I always did the same in that farmhouse, too. Hence, anybody entering would of course be sure to spot me sleeping in the back the very moment they set foot in the place.

It was dusk, and I seem to recall that I had a slight temperature. As I lay there, dozing, I suddenly sensed another person's presence. I hauled myself over in bed and quickly sat up.

There, standing on the earthen floor, I saw a short man of around thirty-five. He had on a *haori* jacket over an Oshima kimono and wore a pair of *hakama*. His hat was perched precariously at the back of his head. In his left hand he carried an Inverness coat, and in his right, a rattan cane. Both the kimono and the *haori* looked rather worn, and, all told, the young man had an altogether shabby appearance, with little to redeem it.

We stared at each other for a few seconds, before I eventually called out from my bed, asking who it was. The young man grinned. He set down his cane and Inverness coat, removed his hat and slowly mopped the sweat on his brow, before asking me whether I was the owner of the house. His cool demeanour set me a little on edge, so I asked him again, and somewhat reproachfully this time, who he was. But the man only grinned once more. Then, with a slight stammer, he introduced himself: 'I-I'm…'

He said, of course, that his name was Kosuke Kindaichi.

I shall spare you the details about how surprised, or rather how alarmed, I was to hear this, but I ought to say a few words about what the name Kosuke Kindaichi meant to me. I was, at the time, in the process of writing a novel based on what I had heard from the locals about a murder that had taken place in the old *honjin* in the village. The novel, moreover, was being serialized in a magazine. But the protagonist of that novel—or, perhaps I should say the protagonist of that case—was none other than Kosuke Kindaichi. Not only had I never met the man, but I had never even seen him before. And, of course, I had written the book without his permission. I had merely based it on what the villagers told me, embellishing their recollections with my own imagination. And yet, this very man had now turned up unannounced on my proverbial doorstep. It should be little wonder then that I was both surprised and alarmed. I could feel the cold perspiration, brought on by a sense of guilt, drip from under my arms. Even when we exchanged greetings after he entered the tatami room, I was at a loss for words.

Kosuke Kindaichi watched me hum and haw, grinning before he offered at last an explanation for his visit.

He was on his way back, he said, from Gokumon Island, a small, isolated spot in the Seto Inland Sea, but before going there, he had paid a visit to a patron of his, a certain Ginzo Kubo, from whom he had heard, much to his surprise, that somebody was writing a novel about him. He had, it transpired, read the novel himself, so, before leaving for the island, he had sent a letter to the magazine, asking for the address of the author, and now, having found the reply waiting for him upon his return, he had made a beeline for the village.

'I've got a bone to pick with you,' he said, smiling amiably.

Hearing the jovial tone in his voice, I finally relaxed. Not only was there not a hint of malice in his words, but there was even a certain affection. Emboldened by this, I asked what he thought of the novel. It was rather presumptuous of me, I must admit, but once again he grinned and said that he thought it was 'spot on'. He said he was flattered that I had painted him in such a complimentary light, but, 'If I could suggest one thing,' he added, 'it would be that you write a little more about what a handsome devil I am!'

He roared with laughter as he scratched the bird's nest of hair atop his head. And so, in short, we hit it off splendidly.

Kosuke Kindaichi stayed with me for three nights, during which time he told me all about his most recent case on Gokumon Island and, moreover, gave me his blessing to

14

write about it. In other words, he adopted me as his official biographer.

Over the course of those three days that he spent with me, we discussed all manner of things having to do with detective novels, and it was then that I broached the subject of the so-called 'faceless corpse' murder. I recall telling him that around twenty years ago I tried to classify all the detective stories in a certain magazine. The magazine is long gone now, so I cannot say with certainty, but I seem to recall observing that the 'double role' type, the 'locked room' type and the 'faceless corpse' type were among the most common ones. Two decades have passed since then—a time in which detective novels have come on by leaps and bounds—but it is interesting to note that to this very day those three archetypes still occupy the top spots in detective writing.

If you scrutinize these three archetypes, you will soon realize that there are significant differences between them, however. That is to say, the 'locked room' mystery and the 'faceless corpse' are challenges set for the readers, who will recognize, almost as soon as they open the book, what kind of mystery awaits them. Yet, the same cannot be said of the 'double role' type. This, instead, is a trick that must be kept secret right until the very end, and, if the readers suspect that the novel is of this kind, then the author has lost the game. (Naturally, in all manner of detective novels, the culprit will seem like a good person, so, while this is

15

a kind of 'double role', it is distinct from the 'double role' type of which I write here.)

In that sense, the 'double role' type is very different from the 'locked room' mystery and the 'faceless corpse', but then those two other types are also very different from each other. This is because the 'locked room' type always presents the same problem, only with an infinite number of solutions; or perhaps I should say that, with this type, what both the author and the reader are interested in is how many different solutions can be offered for the same problem.

That is not true of the 'faceless corpse' type, however. If ever you come across a case in a detective novel in which the face of the body is unidentifiable—that is, a case in which a face has been horribly mutilated, or in which a head has been severed, or in which a body has been discovered in the ruins of a fire that has rendered the features unrecognizable, or even, come to think of it, one in which the whereabouts of the body itself is unknown—in such cases, you can be reasonably sure that the victim and the perpetrator will have switched places. In other words, in most 'faceless corpse' cases, Person A, who is believed to be the victim, will in fact be the murderer, while Person B, who is thought to be the murderer—and who has apparently absconded, of course—will turn out to be the deceased, i.e. the victim. This, with few exceptions, has been the solution offered in most detective novels that have dealt with this theme until now.

'Don't you find it odd?' I said, with a look of triumph on my face, after setting all this out. 'One of the most important conditions for the appeal of a detective novel is the unexpectedness of the ending, yet in every instance of the "faceless corpse" type, the victim and the murderer always trade places. Effectively, from the very outset, the reader always knows who the murderer is. This is a real problem for the author. And yet, despite its disadvantages, most crime authors feel drawn to tackle it at least once in their career. Such is the allure of this problem.'

'So, what you're saying is,' said Kosuke Kindaichi, 'that whenever there's a "faceless corpse" in a detective novel, you can be sure that the victim and the culprit will be confused?'

'Exactly. There will be the odd exception to this rule, but it would appear that authors find the formula of switching more interesting.'

'Hmm,' said Kosuke Kindaichi, as he paused to think. 'But it isn't an incontrovertible fact that this formula is more interesting than the exceptions to the rule, is it? That's simply the case with the novels that have been written until now. It's not inconceivable that someday there'll be an even more interesting "faceless corpse" novel in which the victim and the culprit haven't switched places.'

'That's just what I've been thinking!' I said, leaning forward. 'Say, Kindaichi-san, have you handled any cases like this, ones where the truth has proved stranger than fiction? I may be only a humble writer of detective stories, but one day I'd like to take up this theme and surprise all those mystery buffs with an ending that goes beyond the usual formula.'

As I pictured it, I was practically frothing at the mouth with excitement.

'Well, now, let me see,' said Kosuke Kindaichi, grinning. 'I don't believe I've ever come across anything of the kind before. But please don't be discouraged. All sorts of things do happen. And the world is full of the most inventive people. So, I could well stumble upon a case that fits your aim at any moment. If I do, I promise to let you know about it straight away.'

And so he did, keeping his promise to me.

I shall spare you the details of how thrilled I was when that package arrived, and how I shuddered as I read those documents; otherwise, you readers will start to lose your patience with this rather longwinded introduction of mine.

But there is one more thing that, with your indulgence, I should like to add. As Kosuke Kindaichi mentioned in his letter, these documents were truly a collection of all kinds of records, and I agonized over how best to handle them. I considered laying them out in order, as is often done in foreign novels, but I worried that this would be too confusing for the reader, so in the end I opted to write it in the style of a novel. Whether or not I have succeeded in this endeavour is for you readers to judge.

CHAPTER ONE

G—— Town, where the events of this case took place, is situated outside the Tokyo metropolitan railway's circle line and is in such a far-flung spot that, to get there, you have to get off at Shibuya and then transfer to another line, heading west. The entire neighbourhood is very hilly, with steep slopes wherever you go. According to the elderly residents, there are ninety-nine slopes in all. Even if that number is something of an exaggeration, there are certainly a lot of hills in the area. Perhaps this topography is why this suburb of the capital was late to develop. Until around fifteen years ago, houses there were a rarity, and the place still retained many of the rustic features of old Musashino. But all that had changed in the late thirties, with the start of the so-called China Incident. After a large munitions factory and several subcontracting factories were built in the local area, G——Town suddenly sprang to life. Houses were built one after another, and, in the blink of an eye, the ninety-nine hills were filled up. The roads around G—— Town Station were asphalted, and a shopping precinct was created. Dubious-looking bars and cafes began popping up all over the place. And so, in place of the quaint Musashino of the past, a town far bleaker, drearier and more disorderly came into being.

I do not know how the town changed during the war; however, judging from the newspaper articles that Kosuke Kindaichi sent me, it would seem that while some damage was inflicted, there was none of the total devastation seen elsewhere in the capital. The shopping precinct around the station at least remained intact. What's more, as was the case with all areas that escaped the ravages of war, G—— Town also saw a sharp increase in the number of residents afterwards, and, unlike the rest of postwar Japan, it seemed to enjoy a prosperity even more chaotic and unsavoury than before the conflict.

The shopping precinct was a stretch that ran down the hill directly in front of the station, heading west for about three blocks. All its charm lay in that downward slope: one of the supposed ninety-nine hills, it had been known his-torically as G—— Hill but was now called simply the High Street. Just step off the main drag, however, and you would soon see what a seedy area it really was.

Behind the main street lay warrens of backstreets and alleyways that were commonly known as 'the pink labyrinth' and 'the alleys of temptation'. Come nightfall, these narrow, dark, maze-like streets would be lined on both sides with hundreds of red and violet lanterns, and, in each house, two or three garishly made-up women would stay up till the small hours, playing the gramophone loudly or crooning lewd songs—and occasionally taking turns to disappear upstairs with a man.

What was unique about the place, however, was that even amid this hellish maze of lust and desire, there still remained quite a few vestiges of old Musashino: next door to a bar with its red lantern outside, you might see a thatched cottage or traditional farmhouse, while behind a violet-lit knocking shop (known in the local area as 'cafes'), you could just as easily find an old temple or a graveyard, which added an even more complex and bizarre colour to the local scenery. For the most part, it appeared, this scene had remained unchanged since the war.

It was in one such corner of the town that the incident I am about to relate took place.

It happened just after midnight on the 20th of March 1947. Constable Hasegawa, who had been assigned to the police box on the High Street, was diligently making his rounds of the pink labyrinth.

Ever since the war, the policing of areas like this had become awfully lax, but one benefit of the disrupted transport system and the danger of the city at night was that trading hours were shorter now than they had been in the past. Whereas in former times midnight would have been but the start of the evening, now most of the shopkeepers had already turned out their lights and gone to bed.

That night, Hasegawa was making his way slowly down a meandering hill in the northern part of the town. It was a backstreet commonly known as 'the Back Cut', and it ran through a neighbourhood where the traces of old Musashino were particularly strong—a temple here, a cemetery there—while to the north there was a fairly large area that had been razed during the fire-bombings, lending the place an air of true desolation.

As Hasegawa came ambling along the dark, desolate Back Cut, he suddenly stopped in his tracks and peered down the hill in front of him. From that point on, the hill became steep, and for about twenty yards or so the path seemed almost to fall away, before returning to a gentler incline just as it crossed a road running north–south. If you turned left there and followed the road down, you would come out onto the High Street.

What had caught the policeman's attention was the garden of a property on the left-hand side of the junction. Not only could he see a light flickering there, but he could also hear the telltale sound of somebody digging in the earth. It was little wonder, then, that his chest was pounding.

Hasegawa, who was well familiar with the geography of the area, knew exactly what the building was. It was called the Black Cat Cafe, and it was the sort of establishment that, come evening, would put out a violet lantern. The policeman recalled that, until recently, the Black Cat had been run by a couple who had sold it off only a week ago before moving away. The new owner was still in the process of having the place done up, so at night the building would lie empty.

Remembering this, Hasegawa, with a deep sense of foreboding in his heart, tiptoed down the hill and stole up to the back gate. Then, stooping because the gate was a step lower than the road, he peered in through the gap between the doors, and his heart began to thump all the more violently.

The garden was of modest proportions, certainly no more than 400 square feet. Behind the Black Cat stood an old Buddhist temple called the Renge-in, which belonged to the Nichiren sect. Its grounds stood higher than those of the Black Cat, however, and so the garden was bounded on two sides by a steep bank. And the further away that bank was from the temple, the more it overhung the garden, creating a kind of irregular triangle. The flickering light was coming from the furthest corner of that triangle.

As his eyes became accustomed to the light, Hasegawa saw that there was a paper lantern hanging from a tree on the bank and that there was a person with his back to him, digging in the ground intently. Since the light was coming from the opposite side, the policeman couldn't quite make the figure out, but it looked as though he was wearing a kimono and had tucked the hem of it up at the waist. The figure would pitch the spade into the ground and then, using his foot, stamp down on top of it. Thus was he shovelling the earth away. Why this man was digging a hole in such a place and at such an hour was a mystery, but he was fixated on the task in hand and would pause from time to time only to wipe the sweat from his brow.

The rhythmic sound of the shovel striking the earth continued, and an eerie feeling spread throughout the darkness that hung all around.

'Oh!' The man digging let out a deep groan. He then threw down the spade, got on all fours like a dog, and began rummaging around in the dirt with his hands. His heavy breathing, mixed with the sound of soil flying all over the place, was a sign of just how frantic he was.

'Argh!' The man suddenly let out a shriek and leapt back, as though he had been pushed. He then just stood there, staring timorously at the hole in the ground.

Even in the dark, Hasegawa could see that the man's back was shaking, so he started banging loudly on the gate.

'Open up! Open up!'

However, in the time that it took Hasegawa to shout these words, he realized that it would be quicker simply to climb over the wall. The policeman sprinted a few steps up the hill and, using that momentum, scaled the wall. When he looked inside, he saw the man in question hunched over, looking back at him, but there was no sign that he was about to run away.

'What's going on here? What are you doing?' Hasegawa asked, jumping down from the wall.

The man suddenly stepped back, as though frightened by the sight of the policeman running towards him, and went around to the other side of the hole he had been digging. Only then did the light from the lantern and that from the policeman's torch fall directly on the man's face, allowing Hasegawa to see at last who it was: it was Nitcho, a young monk from the Renge-in.

'Oh, it's you!' said the policeman. 'What on earth are you doing here?'

The monk seemed to want to answer, but his jaw was trembling so much that it was impossible for him to get his words out.

Hasegawa was on the point of repeating the question when he glanced down at the hole by the man's feet. Crying out in fright, he staggered back. Then, as though doubting his eyes, he pointed his torch down and looked again. There, inside it, lay the half-buried body of a woman. It appeared as though the monk had been digging and pulled her partly out. The lower half of her body was still covered in earth, but despite this Hasegawa could tell that it was a woman right away because the corpse itself was naked; and while the upper half was still covered in soil and dirt, the body was lying on its back, and the slight mounds of her breasts were impossible to mistake.

Hasegawa drew the circle of light towards the face of the corpse, but just then he let out an inaudible scream and gripped the handle of his torch so tightly that it very nearly broke. After taking a couple of breaths, Hasegawa instinctively turned to the monk and looked at the damp cloth in his hands. He then looked back at the corpse's face and clutched the handle tighter still. The monk must have dampened the cloth in a nearby puddle and tried to wipe the mud off the face; it looked as though he wanted to find out to whom the body belonged right away, but could anybody have identified that face?

No, you couldn't even call it a face anymore. If anything, you would sooner have called it the remains of what had once been a face. The lips had already decomposed, shrivelling up to reveal the white of bone underneath. The eyes and nose were completely gone, and, where they had once been, there were now just gaping holes, while the little bit of flesh left around them had curled up and hardened to grey. There appeared to be some skin left on the head, and there were a few remaining hairs, wet and stuck down to the remains of the face, but it was impossible to tell whether they belonged to a man or a woman.

This sight of this alone was eerie enough, but what made it even more so were the countless tiny white maggots covering the remains. Because of their ceaseless wriggling, the entire face seemed to flinch in the light of the torch.

Feeling as though he might vomit at any moment, Hasegawa suddenly averted the light of his torch from this appalling sight and turned to Nitcho.

'Wh-what's the meaning of this?' he pressed the monk. 'Whose body is that? And what on earth were you doing digging here?'

Nitcho, in response, moved his lips as though he were trying to speak, but once again his jaw just trembled uncontrollably, making it impossible to understand what he was saying. His ugly face, with its broad, bowl-shaped, deformed skull and two large veins on his dark forehead that were swollen like worms, lent him a sinister air. And then there was the crazed, glazed-over look in his bloodshot eyes. The corpse that had been half-exhumed from the ground was one thing, but Hasegawa found the sight of the youth's face somehow even more terrifying, so much so that he couldn't help looking away.

CHAPTER TWO

This discovery, as I have already mentioned, took place just after midnight on the 20th of March 1947, and after that the investigation began in earnest; however, because of the late hour, the police officers did not arrive at the scene until the early hours of the next morning. Among them was an experienced detective called Murai, and it seems that the first thing he did when he arrived on the scene was to investigate the geography of the neighbourhood. In the bundle of documents that Kosuke Kindaichi sent to me, there was a map that Murai sketched at the time, along with an explanation. According to the map, the neighbourhood around the Black Cat was roughly as follows:

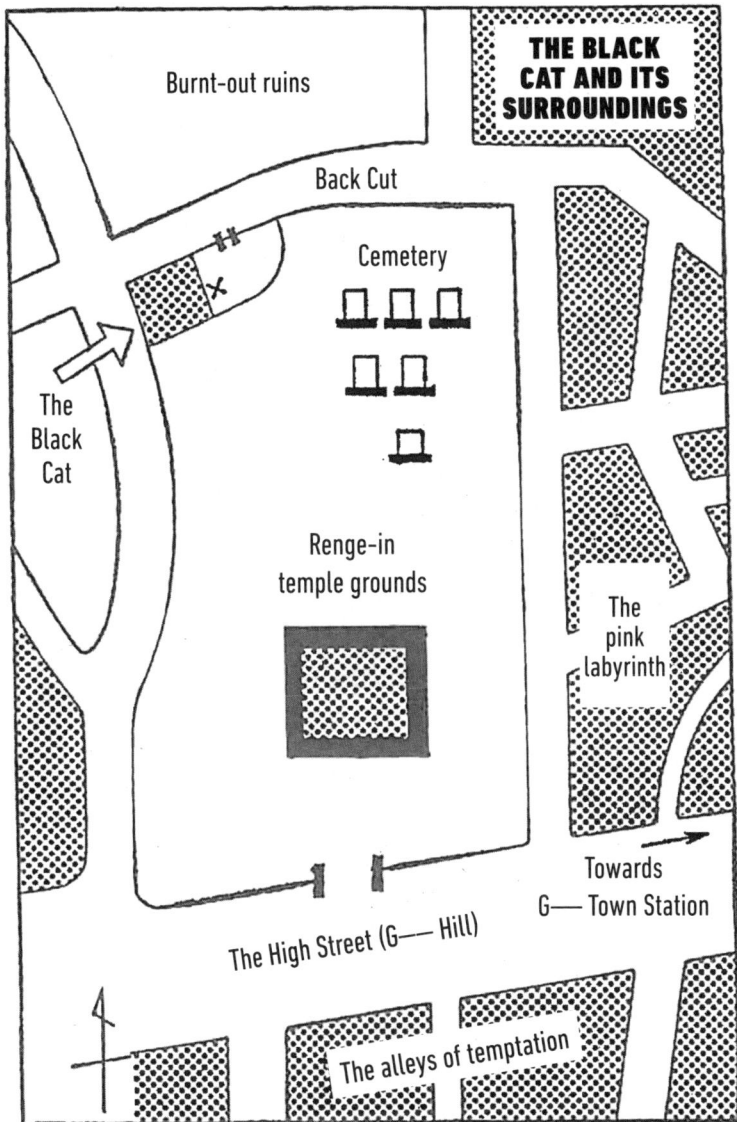

THE BLACK
CAT AND ITS
SURROUNDINGS

Burnt-out ruins

Back Cut

Cemetery

The
Black
Cat

Renge-in
temple grounds

The
pink
labyrinth

Towards
G— Town Station

The High Street (G— Hill)

The alleys of temptation

The Renge-in had seemingly been quite important in the old days, and its large grounds stretched from the High Street all the way to the Back Cut. In other words, the main temple gate was located in the busy shopping precinct, while the rear of the temple, where the Black Cat was located, was surrounded by a wooded area. There was a rather neglected cemetery there, too. As I have already said, the whole area sloped down to the west, but on the western side of the Renge-in—that is, at the back of the Black Cat—there was a big, sudden drop. The steep bank, moreover, extended as far as the street that ran north–south, connecting the High Street with the Back Cut, which meant that the Black Cat was surrounded by these high rockfaces on two sides—namely the south and east. With no neighbouring houses, and with the area to the northwest nothing but a burnt-out wasteland, the Black Cat appeared to stand entirely alone. In terms of geography, it seemed like the perfect spot for a gruesome crime.

Having ascertained all this, Murai entered the back garden of the Black Cat. A preliminary examination had already been carried out, and the body had been taken away for an autopsy. However, on orders from the chief inspector, some of the young officers were still scouring the garden meticulously for evidence.

The detective walked over to the chief inspector.

'What were the results of the post-mortem, sir? Do we know how long she's been dead?'

'About three weeks, apparently. Of course, we can't be sure until we have the results of the autopsy.'

'Three weeks? Today's the 20th, so that would put the murder around the end of last month or the start of this one.'

'Give or take, yes.'

'Has the body been buried here all that time, then? It's a wonder no one noticed it before. According to the neighbours, the previous owners moved out only a week ago. Apparently, in addition to the husband and wife who ran the place, there were three women; I doubt they were all in on it, sir, but I do wonder how it was that they didn't notice. That hole where the body was buried isn't exactly small. And there must be traces of digging left all over the place.'

'The culprit had a plan to cover it up, though. Just look at all that—leaves everywhere. They used them to conceal the hole.'

Murai nodded and looked up. The Black Cat's little back garden was overhung by a coppice of trees belonging to the Renge-in.

'What about the cause of death, sir? It was a murder, wasn't it?'

'Of course it was! And it looks as though she received an almighty blow to the back of the head. That's the murder weapon over there. It was dug up with the body a little while ago.'

The chief inspector pointed to the matting by his feet. There, on the mat, where until only a short while ago the dead body had lain, was a hatchet covered in mud. It was of the small variety that you might find in any suburban household, and it was certainly a convenient and potentially lethal weapon. Murai looked at the dark stains on the blade and the handle and frowned. He then turned suddenly to the chief inspector.

'Sir, what's this hair doing here…? Oh! Is it a wig?'

'Yes, they found it with the body. It would seem that the victim wore a hairpiece. Most women bob their hair nowadays, so, if they want to do their hair up, they have to use something like this.'

'So, it belonged to the victim, then? Is there anything that might help us establish her identity?'

'Nothing. She was stripped naked. All we know is that she was between twenty-five and thirty years old. But, if we look into women from the local area who disappeared around three weeks ago, we should be able to work it out,' the chief inspector said matter-of-factly.

Only later would he realize what a difficult task this was.

'By the way, sir, this monk, Nitcho… How did he know there was a body buried here?'

'How, indeed? The man's awfully het up, and he's in no fit state for questioning yet. But according to what he told Hasegawa last night, the story seems to be something like this: two or three days ago, he happened to be passing along the top of the bank, when he heard some rustling in the garden. He peered down and saw a dog digging around in a pile of leaves, and that was when he saw what looked like a human leg poking up out of the ground. At the time, however, he didn't quite have the courage to come down and check it out. But apparently he just couldn't stop thinking about it afterwards. The more he tried to forget it, the more he could see it in his mind's eye. In the end, he even began seeing it in his dreams, and so that night he decided to come and see for himself. Or at least that's what he said. And look over there. You can see the footprints where he came sliding down the steep bank. He must have come armed with a shovel. What an odd fellow! If he was so worried, he could have gone to the police box, but he said he didn't want to bother them. Of course, he wouldn't have known at that point whether it really was a human leg, but still, it's odd… I'd like you to interview him later. I think he might be a little unhinged. Oh, and— What's going on? Has something happened?'

One of the detectives digging at the foot of the bank had let out a strange cry. The chief inspector rushed over, leaving Murai to follow behind him.

'It's a cat, sir! Look, there's a black cat buried here.'

'A black cat?'

Surprised by this, the chief inspector and Murai peered into the hole that the detective had dug. Sure enough, there, among the leaves and dirt, was the half-buried body of a jet-black cat.

'Shall I leave it buried here, sir?'

'No, you'd better dig it up.'

As the young detective set to work again, a voice came from the side gate: 'Did somebody say "a black cat"?'

It was Hasegawa. He made his way over to the hole in the ground and looked down.

'Oh, it's *the* black cat!'

'*The* black cat? You mean to say you know this cat?'

'Yes, sir. The owners kept it as a sort of mascot, given the name of the place, and all. I wonder when it died… Ah!'

He was not alone in crying out: the men surrounding the hole all gasped in unison, their faces turning pale.

The young detective who had cleared away the surrounding earth scooped up the cat on the blade of the shovel, but, as soon as he did, the cat's head began to dangle precariously: its neck had been cut so perfectly that the head seemed to be hanging by the merest thread, ready to fall off at any moment.

'What a cruel thing to have done!' said Murai.

Even an experienced officer like him couldn't help wincing and rubbing his eyes.

'Hmm,' the chief inspector growled. 'See that you take good care of that cat. It may well have something to do with this case.' Then, turning to Hasegawa, he asked, 'You wouldn't happen to know roughly when this cat disappeared, would you?'

'Now, let me see… Speaking for myself, sir, I don't think I noticed. But… ah, yes! That's right. It was definitely around until five or six days ago. Even after the old owners moved out and the place became vacant, I'd still see a black cat prowling about from time to time.'

'Until five or six days ago?' the detective said.

'Come again?' The chief inspector looked at Hasegawa in amazement. 'Don't be absurd, Constable! Just look at that cat! It's hard to say for sure, but it's clearly been dead for ten, maybe even twenty days.'

'But I *have* seen a cat more recently, sir… How peculiar. You're right enough, though: this cat really has begun to decompose.'

Hasegawa took off his hat, looked down quizzically, and scratched his head in consternation. The chief inspector and Murai traded glances. A strange and terrible feeling passed through their chests. For a moment nobody spoke. But just then, the young detective who had discovered the cat suddenly threw down his shovel and leapt back.

'Whatever's the matter? Have you found something else?'

'O-o-over there! A black cat!'

'What?'

Human emotions are strange things, indeed. Ordinarily, the appearance of a lone black cat would not have startled anyone, but now all of them quite literally jumped in fright. It was just as the young detective had said. From the top of the bank, a jet-black cat with shining amber eyes was watching them intently. Its magnificent glossy black fur stood out among the dead grass with an uncanny sheen.

'Here, kitty-kitty…'

When Murai called to it, the cat emerged from the grass and gave a friendly meow.

'Here, kitty!' Murai purred.

'*Meow!*' the cat replied and came bounding down the bank.

It glanced up at the men gathered there with what seemed like a look of reproach, before running inside the house through the back door.

'So, there were two cats? That must have been the one you saw the other day, Hasegawa.'

'It's difficult to say, sir. They look identical…'

'Hmm… Yes, they're impossible to tell apart when they have black fur. And they're both around the same size. Or could it be that they bought a replacement after the old cat died?'

'It's certainly possible, sir. I'm afraid I neglected to check the family register for cats…'

A witticism like this was out of character for Hasegawa, but it brought a smile to the chief inspector's lips.

'On which note,' he said, 'did you bring the family register with you?'

'Yes, sir, I have it right here. And while I was at it, I also paid a visit to the local council office and did some digging around.'

'Is that so? Well, let's go inside and hear all about it. Murai, give the house a thorough going-over. I suspect the crime must have been committed inside the house—and, if it was, there's bound to be evidence of it left somewhere in there.'

The chief inspector escorted Hasegawa through the back door.

Like most establishments of this kind, the Black Cat had a *tori-niwa*, an earthen-floored passageway that ran the length of the house from the back door to the front. As they stepped inside, there was a modestly sized sitting room with tatami mats immediately to their left; it was the only downstairs room furnished with them (the rest were all earthen), and it looked as though it had been used by the owners as a sitting room. It was separated from the bar at the front by the kitchen.

The chief inspector and Hasegawa made their way through to the bar. The cafe was still being renovated by the new owners, but it was early enough in the morning that the workmen were yet to arrive. There were half-finished boards leaning against the walls here and there, and scraps of wood strewn all over the place.

The chief inspector pulled up a chair and sat down at a table in one corner of the room.

'Take a seat, Constable,' he said. The chief inspector paused, looking expectantly at Hasegawa while the latter made himself comfortable. 'Right, let's hear what you have to say then…'

CHAPTER THREE

'Until about a week ago—or, to be more precise, until the 14th of this month—three people were living here: the owner and his wife, and another woman. And then there were another two who worked here but lived elsewhere…'

Referring to the family register and the copy of the civil register he had found in the council office, Hasegawa went on to explain everything in more or less the following terms. The owners were called Daigo and O-Shige Itojima. According to the family register, Daigo was forty-two, while his wife O-Shige was twenty-nine. They had taken over the cafe in July 1946—that is, in the summer of last year— and, looking at the change-of-residence certificate that Hasegawa had found in the council office, it appeared that Daigo had previously been living in Nagano, while O-Shige had resided separately in Yokohama. Before that, it seemed, they had both been living in China.

'Well, well! So, the two of them are returnees?'

'It certainly looks that way, sir. And here's what I found out about O-Kimi. That's the live-in girl, by the way...'

Daigo Itojima was not the typical kind of man to run a business like this. A little on the portly side, he had a ruddy, kindly face, and he was always smiling. He may not have been the sharpest, and he had a laid-back approach to work, but he still managed everything himself, from bartending to cooking, and from buying in stock to running errands.

As for the proprietress of the Black Cat, O-Shige, she was listed in both the family register and the municipal register as being twenty-nine, but in fact she looked a little older than that. This probably had something to do with her hair.

'Maybe it was having been abroad in the overseas territories for so long that drew her to the style.'

Daigo's wife seemingly always wore her hair in an old-fashioned kind of chignon known as an *icho-gaeshi*, the 'inverted gingko leaf', which she would pair with rather sombre-looking kimonos. She was a handsome woman with fine, slender features, but there was a certain sharpness about her face; it made her look too prim, too aloof, perhaps even a little mean. Ultimately, however, none of the other women in the neighbourhood could hold a candle to her, and so all the patrons of the Black Cat had their sights set on her.

There were, of course, the other girls who worked there: besides the live-in girl, O-Kimi, there were the two girls who would come and go, Kayoko and Tamae. A country girl of only seventeen, O-Kimi still had no experience in the ways of the world—she had not yet even learnt how to apply face powder properly—and, while she did serve in the bar, O-Shige would not let her take any customers. Indeed, it seemed that O-Shige had kept her as a maidservant, and not as that other kind of woman commonly found in the area...

Kayoko claimed to be twenty-three, and Tamae said that she was twenty-two, but there was no guarantee that either of them was telling the truth. They both wore equally garish make-up and equally disgraceful Western clothes, but while Tamae had a figure that made one wonder what all the fuss was about food shortages, Kayoko was as thin as a grasshopper and prided herself on her good looks.

'...so, all five of these people were here at the Black Cat until a week ago.'

'I see. And do we know where they all are now?'

'That shouldn't be difficult, sir. The Itojimas and O-Kimi have obtained change-of-address certificates, while Kayoko and Tamae are due to come back here once the renovation work is complete.'

'Hmm... So, none of them is a match for the body, then?'

Hasegawa's eyes bulged as he stared back at the chief inspector. It looked as though the very notion had never occurred to him.

'Sorry, sir, I should have mentioned. Even since the Itojimas moved out, I've seen O-Kimi, Kayoko and Tamae from time to time. With Kayoko and Tamae, it was on the 14th, the day the Black Cat closed. I ran into them on the street and asked whether they'd had to stop working. They said yes but added that they'd start again just as soon as the bar reopened. They said that the new owner had been keen for them to stay on, or something like that. As for O-Kimi, I saw her the day before that, at the local council office. She'd gone there to get her change-of-address certificate. She said she'd been given the sack, so she was going to stay with her aunt in Meguro.'

'And what about O-Shige?'

'The owner's wife? Now, let me see… Well, sir, you did say that the dead woman had been killed about three weeks ago, didn't you? I'm sure I'd have heard about it if she'd gone missing before she shut the bar on the 14th… Ah, but I'm forgetting. I did run into her just after that. That's right, it was on the evening of the 14th. As you know, sir, my police box is located just as you come out of the side street. I was standing in front of it, you see, and Mr and Mrs Itojima hurried past together. I remember thinking that they were moving out at last, so it must have been the evening of the 14th.'

'Yes, I see. So then, the body can't be that of anyone from the Black Cat… Incidentally, do you happen to know where the Itojimas moved?'

41

'Quite a way away, sir: they've moved to Kobe.'

'Kobe, eh? Hmm…' For a few moments, the chief inspector just sat there, lost in thought, but suddenly he leant in and said, 'One last thing, Constable. This may be the most crucial question of all. Under what pretext did the Itojimas decide to give up the bar? What are the neighbours saying?'

'Well, that's just it, sir. Everybody thought it was a rather odd decision. Of course, businesses like this are always a little murky—they're certainly not as much fun as they seem—but by all accounts the Black Cat was a real hit. So, when people heard they were selling up, it apparently came as quite a shock, not only to the neighbours, but to Kayoko and Tamae as well. Being the only one who lived with the owners, O-Kimi alone seems to have had some inkling of what was going on. But then, there's also what she said when I saw her at the council office.'

As I mentioned earlier, the Itojimas were returnees from China. O-Kimi had no idea where exactly in China they had been, but she said that it was some out-of-the-way part of Northern China. However, when the war ended, all the Japanese had to be repatriated, and so the Itojimas made their way from the northern hinterlands to Tientsin. Whether they got separated along the way or later on when they were being put onto ships, the two of them did not return to Japan together. O-Shige made it back around six months before her husband.

The fate of a woman on her own, without any posses-
sions, a woman who had, moreover, spent a long time in
the overseas territories and had no acquaintances back in
Japan, was probably a foregone conclusion: O-Shige found
her way into a cabaret in Yokohama. However, as she was
quite a looker, and had skills to match, she caught herself
a man soon enough. He was a builder down in Yokohama,
and he was practically bursting with new yen. She took on
the role of this man's mistress and was able, at last, to make
a nest for herself. The only snag was that her husband,
Daigo, eventually returned. O-Kimi did not know the ins
and outs of what happened next, but O-Shige was forced to
leave her wealthy patron, and with the money she received
from him she bought a share of the Black Cat.

'Seemingly, however, the reality was that O-Shige didn't
make a clean break with her lover. Until recently, she would
meet him from time to time, and, when her husband found
out about this, there was trouble. Even so, O-Shige continued to meet her lover, and her husband was in no position
to do anything about it. After all, it was only because of
his wife that these penniless returnees could put food
on the table. And besides, the husband had a woman of
his own...'

'Oh? And who was that?'

'She was another returnee from China, sir. As I mentioned, Daigo returned to Japan a little after his wife did,
and it seems that he met this woman on board the boat

43

back. Apparently, they lived together for a time while Daigo was trying to find his wife. And not only that, sir, but there are rumours that, even after he and his wife were reunited, he continued to see this woman from time to time.'

'I take it you learnt all this from O-Kimi?'

'That's right, sir.'

'But how did O-Kimi come by all these details, I wonder?'

'She heard it all from Mrs Itojima. O-Shige was using her as her spy, you see. There was one time, apparently, when she ordered O-Kimi to follow Daigo and find out where he was meeting this woman.'

'So, O-Shige was fully aware of this woman's existence, then? Hmm. What happened when she sent O-Kimi to follow him?'

'O-Kimi was very proud of herself for that, sir. If I remember rightly, it happened something like this…'

Owing to all the recent shortages of food and drink, the Black Cat would often find itself having to close for business, and it was then that O-Shige would inevitably head out on her own. Needless to say, it was her lover that she was off to see. Knowing this full well, her husband, who would be left back at home, would always fall into a black mood. Not ordinarily a man to use harsh words, he would gulp down sake by the litre and lash out at O-Kimi. There would always be an argument when O-Shige returned home. But one day Daigo's attitude suddenly changed. When his wife went out, he started to grow restless and began to

44

head out himself. O-Kimi thought this was strange: there was definitely something odd about the master's behaviour. She informed her mistress of this discreetly, whereupon a thought seemed to occur to O-Shige. 'Next time I go out and he does likewise,' she said, 'follow him.'

'So, that's just what she did, sir.'

'And she saw him with another woman? Who was she, this other woman?'

'I understand that she was in her mid-twenties. Very flashily dressed. She made quite the impression, apparently: bobbed hair, heavy lipstick, might have been taken for a dancer or a chorus girl. Daigo met her at Shinjuku Station, where they caught a train to Inokashira and ducked into a strange-looking house. All this O-Kimi reported back to O-Shige. Furious and frustrated, O-Shige said that it must have been Ayuko, a woman who formerly worked at the Sunshine Dance Hall and with whom her husband had travelled back to Japan. "Damn it," she said. "He still hasn't broken it off with her." And so that night, an almighty row erupted between O-Shige and her husband. And it didn't end there. From then on, things took a turn for the worse and there was constant strife between the couple. Sooner or later, O-Shige began to reflect on her predicament. "Well," she said, "I think we ought to put an end to all this." She apparently used to say that she didn't mind being poor, so long as she and her husband lived happily together. But what with all the problems they'd had since coming back to

Tokyo, staying together was hopeless. She said she wanted to go somewhere far away. That was when he announced all of a sudden that he was closing the place. O-Kimi said she wasn't all that surprised.'

For a few moments, as he arranged all the details in his mind, the chief inspector said nothing. The scenario itself was nothing new: it was a common enough story among people like this. But even so, a curious chill ran through the chief inspector. He could not help thinking that, beneath the surface, there lurked some peculiar darkness.

'This mistress of Daigo's, this Ayuko, you said she worked at the Sunshine Dance Hall, is that right? What about O-Shige's lover?'

'His name's Shunroku Kazama, and he's the boss of the Kazama Construction Group.'

The chief inspector made a note of the name in his pocketbook.

'Well, Constable, I think I've got a pretty good idea of the situation in the Itojima household. Although I do wonder about this Nitcho fellow. There's something not quite right about him, don't you think?'

'He is well known for being a little eccentric, if that's what you mean, sir. But then, he has his master to think about. You see, the Renge-in is quite important in these parts. All the land around here, including this land, belongs to the temple. There used to be a lot of monks there, but all of them were drafted into the army and either died in battle or else haven't yet returned, so now there are only two of them in that enormous temple: Nitcho and the old master, Nissho. Nitcho is still quite young—I'd imagine he must be in his mid-twenties—so, by rights, he ought to have been drafted, but he avoided it because he had polio as a child and was left with a bad leg. That said, ever since before the war, old Nissho has been afflicted with palsy, and he is practically bedridden these days. So, never mind all the things Nitcho has to do for his parishioners, he also does everything from washing and cooking to collecting rents. You must understand, though, he's the quiet type. A man of few words—speaks rarely and only when necessary. Still, there's no denying it: given the sort of area this is, the establishments where the rent has to be collected are all of a certain nature, so to speak. Some of the women even make advances on him half-jokingly, but it's no use, of course. Nitcho's quirks have become something of a local legend. He may be a little eccentric, sir, but I think he's harmless enough.'

Just then the front door rattled. Realizing that the workmen had arrived, the chief inspector got to his feet and told them to go around to the back of the property, whereupon he himself made his way there, too, but via the *tori-niwa*.

'Excuse me, Chief Inspector?'

Murai's face appeared from the tatami room at the back.

'Ah, Murai! Have you found anything?'

The chief inspector removed his shoes and stepped up into the sitting room. Without a word, Murai pulled back a thin *usuberi* mat that had been pushed up against the wall. When he saw what lay beneath it, the chief inspector gulped. There on the tatami, hidden by the mat, were sticky traces of blood that looked as though somebody had tried to clean them up.

'So, it was here that the crime was committed, then?'

Murai nodded, then pointed to the tatami mat in front of the built-in wardrobe just behind the *engawa* veranda that faced out onto the back garden.

'If you look at the tatami mat over here, sir, you can clearly see the indents where a chest of drawers stood. Only, why would anybody place a chest of drawers in front of a built-in wardrobe? I believe these two mats must have been swapped recently. But even so, take a look at this, sir…'

A sheet of newspaper had been pasted to the sliding door of the wardrobe, just below the handle.

'I had a job getting it off, but I just about managed it, in the end.'

Murai gingerly picked up a corner of the paper to reveal a dark bloodstain soaked into the wood.

'It's only a working hypothesis, but I imagine there was a struggle between the victim and her assailant in this room. The victim then tried to escape into the garden but was struck from behind with the hatchet. Apropos of which, just look at the date on the newspaper: the 27th

48

of February. Nobody would ever leave the blood smeared over the wardrobe door like that for all to see, so the crime must have taken place on the 27th at the latest. Then again, they'd probably have used whatever newspaper was closest to hand, so I suppose it could have happened a little after that, as well. The paper might not have been that day's, in which case the murder would have taken place on or a little after the 27th, up to, say, the 2nd or the 3rd.'

'Well, that would certainly be consistent with the body's state of decay. But then, that would mean that the Itojimas were living with the corpse of a woman they'd killed for around two weeks.'

As he contemplated the inhumanity of this couple, which defied description, a chill ran down the chief inspector's spine.

CHAPTER FOUR

The chief inspector proceeded to question the workmen, but they seemingly knew nothing. The Itojimas had moved out of the Black Cat on the 14th, but the workers themselves had been coming to the property ever since the day after that. Hence, that day was already their sixth there, but in that time they had encountered nothing out of the ordinary. What's more, they claimed to have not the least inkling as to the identity of the deceased—and that certainly appeared to be the truth of the matter.

While the workmen were being questioned, the new owner, a certain Shozo Ikeuchi, happened to arrive on the scene, but he too was unable to supply any facts that might be of use to the investigation.

This Ikeuchi fellow ran a similar kind of establishment in Shibuya, and he had bought the place after coming across an advertisement for it in the newspaper. He stated that the advertisement had appeared in the classified section of the *Y*—— newspaper on the 7th of March, and that his negotiations with the previous owners had concluded on the 12th. This was immediately checked with the newspaper in question, and no discrepancies were found in Ikeuchi's story.

'So, you'd never had any dealings with the Itojimas before?'

'No. I met Mr Itojima for the first time only after seeing the ad in the paper.'

'And it was Mr Itojima who handled the negotiations? Not his wife?'

'Yes. I never did meet Mrs Itojima…'

After the negotiations had begun, Ikeuchi had made rounds of the neighbourhood, asking about the Black Cat and its reputation locally. It was during these that he heard about O-Shige's beauty and decided that he would like to meet her. But Mrs Itojima was ill and laid up in bed, he was regretfully informed, and so in the end he never got the chance to do so. Before the negotiations were concluded, Mr Itojima gave him a tour of the premises, but even then O-Shige remained shut up in the tatami room and never showed her face. As he listened to all this, the chief inspector nodded to himself: O-Shige must have been in such a panic that she was unable to maintain her composure in front of the prospective buyer. Or so the chief inspector thought. It never occurred to him that there might be another, even more terrible truth lurking behind this.

Be that as it may, the chief inspector was able to learn the addresses of Kayoko and Tamae from Ikeuchi, and so that afternoon the two girls were called in for questioning. At the same time, O-Kimi, who had gone to stay with her aunt in Meguro was also summoned to provide a witness statement. When their three stories were collated, the following tale emerged.

It was on the 13th that Daigo Itojima informed them that the Black Cat was being sold. However, since Ikeuchi had paid several visits to the establishment by then, the girls had a rough idea of what was going on, so the news did not come as much of a shock. After that, Daigo immediately called the clearance firm on the High Street and sold off everything that was of any value. The seller's men came that day and the next to take all the items away. Then, just after midday on the 14th, Kayoko, Tamae and O-Kimi said a final farewell to Daigo and left. They all claimed never to have seen or heard from him again after that.

'So, none of you said goodbye to Mrs Itojima?' the chief inspector asked casually.

The three women looked at each other in embarrassment. Squirming, Kayoko eventually answered, 'Well, you see, officer, it might seem strange, thinking back on it now, but she took unwell back at the start of the month, and ever since then she'd shut herself away in the tatami room and never ventured out of it. To be honest, I thought it was a little odd, even at the time, but I didn't pay it much notice. But, now that you mention it, I don't think any of us saw her even once this month. Even when things were quiet and I said I wanted to pop in and see how she was getting on, Mr Itojima would always say that she hadn't yet recovered and so it was better not to…'

When he heard this, the chief inspector felt a curious unease rise up through his chest. He was unable to pinpoint the reason for it, but it was as if some strange, dark sense of foreboding were spreading through his veins like black ink.

'But can you be sure that she was really there?'

'Oh, yes. We may not have seen her, but we would sometimes catch a glimpse of her from behind when she went to the toilet. And when you passed by the room, you could see her silhouette through the sliding paper door as she lay there or read.'

'What was it that she was ill with, exactly? And if she was that ill, didn't anybody call for a doctor?'

'No. It wasn't that kind of illness, you see. Mr Itojima said that she'd had an allergic reaction to her make-up and that her face had swollen up like some monster's in a fairy tale. That's why she apparently didn't want anybody to see her. She would occasionally have allergic reactions like this. She had one last year, in fact, but this one was much worse.'

Again, the chief inspector could not shake that odd feeling.

'So, when did Mrs Itojima stop showing her face? Do you remember the exact date?'

O-Kimi replied that it was on the 28th of February—that is, the last day of the previous month, a day on which the cafe had to close temporarily. Having been given the day off, O-Kimi had gone to visit her aunt in Meguro, where she spent the night before returning. It was then that Daigo had told her about O-Shige's predicament and asked her not to go into the tatami room. She never saw the mistress's face after that…

O-Kimi's story matched Murai's hypothesis exactly. The murder must have taken place on the 28th of February. Since the Black Cat had been closed that day, Kayoko and Tamae would not have been there, and so that terrible episode would have happened after O-Kimi left.

At this point, the chief inspector decided to change tack and broach the matter of the cat. When he mentioned that the body of a black cat had been dug up at the foot of the bank in the back garden, the three women looked at each other in surprise. It was Kayoko who eventually broke the ensuing silence.

'Come to think of it, I do recall something now. The cat showed up last year, so it was very tame. But for a couple of days at the beginning of the month it was acting very oddly and kept hiding under the veranda. On the third day, Mr Itojima put a string about its neck and tied it to one of the pillars. When I asked him what he was doing, he said that the cat was in heat.'

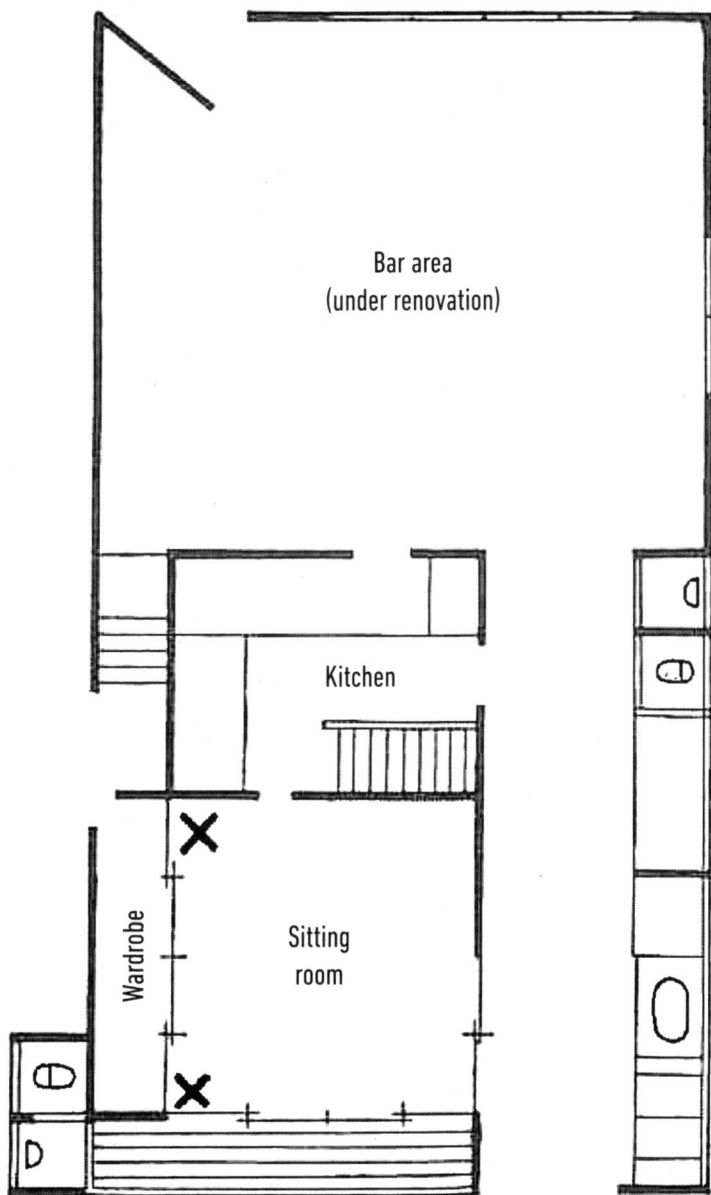

Bar area
(under renovation)

Kitchen

Wardrobe

Sitting
room

'Yes, now that you mention it, I remember that, too,' Tamae piped up. 'I noticed at the time that the cat had suddenly got smaller and said as much to Mr Itojima, but he just laughed and said that when cats are in heat, they lose weight because they don't eat. He said that lust wears out both body and soul. But thinking about it now, he must have been lying. It was a different cat, wasn't it?'

'And Mr Itojima was trying to hide that from us?' asked O-Kimi.

A deathly silence fell over the group. Something terrible had shaken the women and turned their lips cold.

The time had come, at last, to touch on the most important question.

'You will no doubt be aware,' the chief inspector began, 'of the recent discovery at the Black Cat. I would like to hear your thoughts as to the identity of the body we have uncovered. We believe that the murder took place most likely on the 28th of February, so, with that in mind, do you have any ideas?'

The three women exchanged frightened glances.

'Well,' ventured O-Kimi, timidly breaking the silence, 'it's possible that it's... Ayuko... She was...'

'Ah, yes. I'm aware who this is. If I'm not mistaken, she was Mr Itojima's mistress. But why do you believe the body to be Ayuko's?'

'Because Mrs Itojima hated her so very much, and...'

'And? Is there another reason?'

'Er, yes... It's only just come back to me, but... Ah, that's right, it was on the 1st of the month, the morning after we had the day off. It was early; I'd just got back from my aunt's, and I was cleaning up in the bar. Then, under one of the corner tables—you see, there's a little shelf under each of them, where customers can put their things—well, under the table I found a lady's parasol. It was quite a flashy one. It wasn't Mrs Itojima's, and it didn't belong to Kayoko or Tamae either, so, wondering who might have left it there, I decided to open it up, and that's when it hit me. I'd seen this parasol before. It was Ayuko's, I'm sure of it. You see, I'd seen her out walking with Mr Itojima once, and that was definitely the parasol I'd seen her carrying.'

The chief inspector leant in.

'Hmm,' he said. 'So, Ayuko came here while everybody else was out? What did you do with the parasol afterwards?'

'Well, I... When I realized it was Ayuko's, I suddenly got scared and put it back where I'd found it. If I let it slip to Mr Itojima, he'd know that I'd followed him, and if Mrs Itojima got wind of it, there'd be a terrible row, so I pretended I hadn't seen it. But then...'

'But then?'

'Well, it's just that I had to go out to run an errand after that, and by the time I came back the parasol was gone.'

'So, your hypothesis is that this Ayuko came on the 28th and was killed by Mrs Itojima?'

'Oh! There's something I've remembered, too.' It was Tamae who had interjected, and she sounded rather excited. 'Yes, that's right, it was on the 1st of the month—the day after my day off. I don't recall why, but I do remember going out into the garden at the back. That's when I spotted that somebody had been digging there. I asked Mr Itojima about it later and he said he'd wanted to try his hand at growing vegetables, so he'd started to dig but then realized that the spot didn't get much sunlight, so he'd given up...' Tamae looked as if she was on the verge of tears. 'So, her body must have been right under the spot where I was standing, even then.'

She looked down at her feet, as though in disgust.

'So, Mr Itojima admitted to having dug the hole himself?'

Tamae nodded, her face as white as a sheet.

'It might have been Mrs Itojima who killed Ayuko,' she added, 'but it was her husband who buried the body, that's for sure. Ayuko might have been Mr Itojima's mistress, but his wife was the one he truly cared for. That's why he must have buried the body—to protect his wife.'

Neither Kayoko nor Tamae knew all that much about Ayuko. Naturally, they had heard about her from O-Kimi, just as they had heard of O-Shige's jealousy towards her, but they had never met her in the flesh. The only one to have ever seen her was O-Kimi—this was at the end of January—but all she knew about Ayuko was her name and what O-Shige had let slip: that Ayuko had returned from

China together with Daigo, and she had worked at the Sunshine Dance Hall.

'That's right, officer, she'd been working as a dancer,' O-Kimi said. 'She looked the type, too, with those loud Western clothes of hers... Her face? Hmm... I couldn't get too close because Mr Itojima was with her, but she had very attractive features. Ah, yes, and if I'm not mistaken, she had a beauty spot just below her lip, on the right. Whether it was real or not, I couldn't say, but it was quite prominent.'

Lastly, the chief inspector asked them about the recent relations between the Itojimas.

According to the women, Daigo was a gentle sort of man, forever with a smile on his face, but still, they thought there was something creepy about him. O-Shige had always seemed a little afraid of him, too, they said. Apparently, she had begun seeing her lover again on her husband's orders, so that she could rinse him for money, but of course O-Shige was in love with him, and so, even though Daigo was the one sending her out to meet the man, he would always go into a foul mood when she left. Recently, however, he seemed to have got himself involved again with this Ayuko woman, and, whenever O-Shige went out, he would always be anxious to slip out after her. Then it was O-Shige's turn to fly into a temper, which she would take out on Daigo. At any rate, they were an undoubtedly odd couple.

As the chief inspector interviewed these women, Murai had been sitting in a corner of the room the whole time, listening silently. Not even once had he tried to interject. Even after the interview was over and the women had gone home, he just sat there in deathly silence, lost in thought.

For a while, the chief inspector, too, said nothing as he read over his notes, but eventually he turned to Murai and said, 'Effectively, Ayuko is the real question here. Even if we set aside whether or not she's the victim—and, in all probability, I think she is—we'll have to investigate her thoroughly.'

Murai nodded without saying a word.

'It shouldn't be hard,' the chief inspector continued. 'After all, you've been to the Sunshine Dance Hall before, haven't you? If you make enquiries there, you'll be sure to find out.'

Once again, Murai simply nodded. 'And then there's this Kazama fellow,' he added. 'I'll need to look into him as well, sir.'

'Yes. After all, he appears to have been a source of income for O-Shige, doesn't he? Although it won't be plain sailing with somebody as influential as him. Make sure you tread carefully. In the meantime, I'll try to locate the Itojimas. That line about having gone to Kobe is sure to be an out-and-out lie. But then, we don't have much else to go on. It would be better if we had a photo…'

Having been repatriated only recently, the couple had not found time to take even a single photograph. It was only later that the police would realize the bearing this had on the case.

'But, Chief Inspector,' said Murai after a few moments of what seemed to be indecision, 'there's something I can't help wondering about. Why was O-Shige so determined to hide her face? I can well imagine that, after committing such a terrible murder, she might have had a guilty conscience and feelings of dread that made her so ill that she had to take to bed. But two weeks is a long time. And during all that time she never once let those girls see her? Whatever for? Why such caution?'

'Hmm, yes. That struck me as odd, too. But what if, during Ayuko's murder, she was injured herself? Ayuko could have scratched her face, for example…'

Murai nodded. 'That's certainly a possibility, sir. But…'

'But…?'

Murai did not finish the thought. Instead, he changed the subject abruptly.

'Another thing I can't explain is that cat. Why was it killed?'

'What's that? Oh, I suppose it must have got injured while the murder was taking place. Then it was killed so as not to arouse the girls' suspicion. Seemingly there was cat's blood mixed up in the bloodstains left in the other room, so that would appear to confirm this.'

Murai looked as though he wanted to say something but thought better of it.

'Well, at any rate, sir, our first priority is to find out more about this Ayuko. I'll get on it, right away.'

Taking his cap, Murai stood up and left the room.

CHAPTER FIVE

The period from then until the 26th of March, the fateful day when the terrible truth of the matter would come to light and the case would be turned upside down entirely, was one of relative chaos for the police investigation, and one, for Detective Murai, of wrestling with a nagging sense that something was not quite right. Still, there were various things of significance among the pieces of information that Murai had managed to collect during this time, so let us take a moment to examine them now.

At the Sunshine Dance Hall, people remembered Ayuko. She had worked there for a very brief period, however, and during that window she was forever taking time off, so nobody there knew much about her. They did know her surname, though. Ayuko Kuwano—that was her name at the dance hall, but, of course, whether it was real or not, no one could say for sure.

According to the manager, she had worked there for a month, from May until June of last year. She had not come through a connection to the place but had seen an advertisement in a newspaper. When they auditioned her, she had such superb footwork that they did not hesitate to take her on. She paid for her own costumes and accessories, which made life much easier for her employer, and so they did not go to the trouble of making background checks. Everybody knew that she had recently returned from China, however, although nobody could say where or when they had heard this.

'Now let me see… She must have been about 5'2". Her face? Hmm, it's difficult to say. She was certainly a good-looking woman. She wasn't much of a talker, but she had a certain charm that people found attractive… Yes, that's right. I would say her disposition was cheerful, if anything, and she had quite striking features… A beauty spot? Yes, come to think of it, she did have one. Although it was fake. She'd draw it on herself. Then again, it did rather suit her… She was only here for a month, though, and very often she'd call in sick, so I'm afraid that's about all I remember.'

It transpired, however, that the manager was able to find a dancer who had known Ayuko a little better.

'Ayuko? Yes, I remember her. She had a boyfriend. I don't know whether the manager knew about it, but he used to come and pick her up at the stage door. He was a good bit older than she was, so I remember him well. Yes, that's right, he would have been around forty, a little on the heavy side, with ruddy cheeks and a smile that never left his face. Ayuko once told me how he'd really helped her out or something on the boat back from China. No, I've no idea where she went after she stopped working here.'

Another of the dancers had something a little different to say, however.

'Oh, Ayuko? I saw her not so long ago, as it happens. When? It would have been about two months ago, maybe. Around New Year's, I think. I bumped into her just outside the National Theatre. She was with that man of hers. Yes, that's him! The one who used to wait for her at the stage door. Well, anyway, we didn't really speak much, but I understand that she was living somewhere near Asakusa. Incidentally, Kuwano can't have been her surname. I don't think Ayuko was her real name either, in fact. Why? Because she had a suitcase that she brought back with her from China. She was always saying it was the only thing she did bring back. It was monogrammed with the initials C.O.'

Essentially, all he learnt from the Sunshine Dance Hall was that Ayuko and Daigo had seemingly met there often, and that Ayuko's real name apparently began with the initials C.O. Nevertheless, Murai was satisfied with this outcome. He was especially pleased that he now had a clue about her real name.

He then headed for Yokohama.

The sign on the door of the makeshift office read: KAZAMA CONSTRUCTION GROUP. Shunroku Kazama was not at all the man Murai had expected to find there. Given his profession, the detective had envisioned an older, slipperier type, yet, somewhat to his surprise, the man he found was in his mid-forties, had a close-cropped head of hair and still retained some of his youthful looks.

It was a different story when Kazama opened his mouth, however. His mature manner of speaking carried a certain weight, and there was a sharpness to it that could be intimidating, even when he was trying to be conciliatory, yet at the same time he had the polish and sophistication to keep it in check.

Be that as it may, what surprised Murai first was the fact that this man already knew about the discovery in G—— Town, which he let slip rather casually.

'A girl called O-Kimi telephoned to let me know. I've been waiting for one of your lot to show up ever since.'

'I see... Well, perhaps it's for the best that you already know. So, tell me: what do you make of it all?'

'What do I make of it? Hmm. Well, it was certainly a shock to hear what O-Kimi had to say, but the shock soon passed. When I thought about it rationally, I realized it wasn't really all that surprising.'

'By which you mean to say that you had a feeling something like this might happen?'

'Oh, no, nothing like that. All I'm saying is that it's very much in keeping with the times we live in. And besides, isn't that the sort of thing that happens in places like the Black Cat? I mean, bloody cases like that aren't exactly a rarity.'

'Have you ever been to the Black Cat, Mr Kazama?'

'Never. I'm not sure I even know where exactly G—— Town is. I'm hardly liable to go somewhere I'll run into her husband, now, am I?'

Kazama burst out laughing. A man of robust build, he had a deep and resonant voice that suggested a strong pair of lungs.

'Would you mind telling me the nature of your relationship with Mrs Itojima?'

'Of course not. We were neither of us saints. There's no point pretending otherwise. But there's nothing unusual about it, either.'

Kazama met O-Shige for the first time at a certain cabaret in Yokohama at the end of the year before last. She had just returned from China with only the clothes on her back. There were plenty of other women in this cabaret, but it was the sight of O-Shige that so captivated Kazama.

'It was because she would always wear a kimono. Yes, and she would do her hair in that gingko style and tie it up with a band of black satin. It was unusual to see a woman dressed like that in such a place, and that's when I knew I had to talk to her. I didn't have any ulterior motive, though—and that's the truth. Maybe it's a little odd to say so, but women don't hold much interest for me. I've got nothing against them, of course, it's just that I much prefer making money.'

Be that as it may, Kazama ultimately decided to look after the woman.

'In other words, she played me for a fool!' he said, laughing again with that deep, resonant voice of his.

At that time, Kazama's house had been lying empty, so he invited O-Shige to stay there, and every now and then he would pay her a visit. On the whole, he was rather ambivalent about the woman, and so the relationship carried on out of sheer habit.

'So, when her husband came back on the scene, I wasn't all that surprised, to be honest. It would have been around June last year. His name is Daigo. I don't know what you make of him—he may well seem the gentle, peaceable sort—but he's a real piece of work. He had a thing or two to say to me, I can tell you!'

As he said this, a menacing smile appeared on Kazama's lips.

'But, honestly, there was really no need for him to play the tough guy. Frankly, that woman was becoming unmanageable. I shouldn't say this too loudly: I know she spent a long time abroad, and all, but that woman picked up some pretty strange tastes out there, if you catch my meaning.'

Kazama grinned suggestively and then, as if to brush the comment aside, roared with laughter.

'You must forgive me for having led my story down such an unexpected path. But you must understand, I'm an ordinary man of simple tastes. So, while it might have been novel to begin with, it was all too much for me in the end. I decided to end it as soon as possible. Truly, it was a godsend when her husband showed up. I was only too glad to give her back to him.'

'But even so,' said Murai, staring intently at Kazama's face, 'you carried on meeting her afterwards.'

'Well, when you put it like that. What can I say? At the end of the day, a man has his needs. I did try to give her back, you know. And besides, she was the one who came after me. You may well laugh at me for saying this, but it wasn't me that she was interested in. It was all my new yen. What's a man to do?'

'But surely that can't be the whole story. Perhaps she was madly in love with you?'

Murai was able to suggest this quite naturally. While Kazama was speaking, the detective could not help but feel the bold and powerful charisma of the man. It was the type of personality that could drive some women wild. Kazama, however, just smiled wryly without saying a word.

Murai then changed the subject and asked about Ayuko. At the mention of her name, Kazama's brow suddenly darkened.

'I was just thinking about her. No, I never met the girl. But I would hear her name from O-Shige from time to time. O-Shige didn't love her husband. No, she hated him, if anything. But when a woman's husband takes a mistress, her feminine pride won't allow it. How she would complain to me! I wasn't in the least interested in that sort of thing, though, so I always batted it away. But then, the last time I saw her—it would have been mid-February, yes—O-Shige was strangely agitated. One minute she would come out with something morbid like, "I could die at any moment, and when I do, you will offer a stick of incense, won't you?" while the next minute, she'd lose her temper and say, "No, I'm not going to die now, but when I do, I'm taking her with me. Do you think I'd leave her behind?!" She was completely out of control. Looking back on it now, I think she had already made up her mind to do it.'

'Then, you, too, believe that O-Shige was the one who killed Ayuko?'

'Of course. Daigo's hardly going to have killed his own mistress, is he? Personally speaking, I wouldn't be surprised if O-Shige killed someone. She's no lady, that one. She's a real bitch.'

As he said this, there was a menacing grin on Kazama's face.

Once again, Murai changed the subject of discussion. He asked when exactly Daigo had appeared on the scene. Then, much to his surprise, Kazama provided not only the date, but also the name of the ship on which O-Shige's husband arrived.

'It was last April. He arrived on the *Y—— Maru*, which docked at Hakata. O-Shige had come back in the October of the previous year, so that would have been six months after her return. The reason I remember it so distinctly is that I had an acquaintance who was travelling on the same ship.'

As he listened to this, Murai's heart began to pound. He asked whether Kazama would introduce him to this acquaintance of his.

Kazama looked at the detective in surprise, and said, 'Ah, yes, of course. This Ayuko was also on board that ship, wasn't she? Very well…'

Kazama took one of his business cards and, having scribbled a few words of introduction on the back of it, handed it to Murai.

'You must understand, Detective, that I have nothing at all to do with this murder case. However, that's no guarantee that something important won't come up. If it does, come and see me anytime. I always take responsibility for my actions.'

Murai accepted the business card and left the office.

That another person who had travelled back on board that same ship had been identified was a real boon for Murai's investigation. Armed with Kazama's business card, he paid the man a visit the very next day. Only, the man did not recall all that much about Daigo or Ayuko, and so the detective obtained a letter of introduction from this new man and went out in search of other repatriates. In this way, over several days he visited a variety of people who had been carried back to Japan on board the *Y—— Maru*, but in the end all Murai learnt was the following.

The girl with whom Daigo had voyaged back was called Chiyoko Ono, and she had travelled alone from Manchuria to North China, reaching Tientsin just before the ship set sail, so nobody knew her background. Even before boarding the ship, Daigo and the girl had been inseparable, and he had been looking after her in various ways. He was so kind to her, in fact, that those who did not know him thought that they had been together for a long time. Naturally, they were still together when they disembarked in Japan, and seemingly they headed for Tokyo. This much was known, but what happened to them afterwards was a complete mystery. As if this were not disappointing enough, what frustrated Murai was the fact that it was doubtful whether these people would now be able to identify Chiyoko Ono, even if she were put right in front of them. This was because the girl not only cut her hair short and dressed like a man, but she would also smear her face with dirt and soot so that nobody could say what she really looked like. All they knew was that she was in her mid-twenties.

'But isn't all that a moot point, anyway? Even if they did remember the girl's face, the corpse is rotting beyond recognition, so there's no way they'd be able to identify her.'

'Yes, I suppose you're right enough, sir,' came Murai's half-hearted reply to the station chief. 'So, did you manage to find anything on the Itojimas' whereabouts?'

'I'm afraid we've reached something of a dead end with that. We've no idea where they went after they passed the police box in G—— Town. They seem to have just vanished, damn it. I don't suppose that Kazama chap could be hiding them, out of some bizarre sense of chivalry, could he?'

'I doubt it, sir… After all, what possible reason could he have to do that?'

Thus several days passed without any further progress. But then the 26th, that fateful day of revelations, arrived…

CHAPTER SIX

On the morning of the 26th, one of the labourers working on the renovations at the Black Cat, a carpenter by the name of Tamekichi Eto, showed up at the police station and made the following statement:

'I only heard about this last night, you see, and I thought it was a little odd, which is why I'm bringing it up with you now. That's right, yes, last night. I'd already heard that it was Nitcho from the Renge-in who dug up the body. But it's the reason that he was digging that's odd. Apparently, he'd seen a dog digging around two or three days before that, and what looked like a human leg sticking up out of the ground. And that's why he decided to go digging that night? As I say, I only heard about this last night, but can that really be true?'

The questioning way in which Tamekichi was speaking made the station chief, the chief inspector and Murai all feel somewhat tense. What he had said was correct, how-ever. Or at least that was what Nitcho had said. When they told Tamekichi as much, the labourer pulled a wry face.

'But that can't be right. There has to be some mistake. You see, the day before the body was dug up—it must've been late in the afternoon on the 19th—I made a bonfire in the garden, and so I had to rake up all the fallen leaves. Only, since all this has happened, Mr Hasegawa—that is, Police Constable Hasegawa—told me where and how exactly the body was buried. He even pointed it out to me, so I know exactly where the leg was supposed to be sticking up. But the thing is, I'd raked up all the leaves that were lying in that spot on the evening of the 19th, and there definitely wasn't any leg poking up out of the ground...'

The three police officers gulped when they heard this.

'You... you're... quite sure about this?' the chief inspec-tor asked, flustered.

'There were an awful lot of leaves there, sir. So, supposing there had been a leg sticking up among them: just think how much it would have to be poking out of the ground to be seen from all the way up at the top of the bank. And even if my eyes missed it, I'd have still felt the rake come up against something if it had been there. I'll tell you straight-up: there was no leg or arm or anything there on the night of the 19th.'

Needless to say, the police sent for Nitcho directly after Tamekichi left.

'So, how do you explain this? Tamekichi was adamant on this point, and I very much doubt that a dog would be so kind as to fill in a hole and cover it over with leaves again...'

Finding himself suddenly at the sharp end of the station chief's attention, Nitcho looked around at all the men, his eyes glittering. With his broad forehead, sunken cheeks and sickly pallor, the youth had always looked somewhat deformed, but in recent days his cheekbones seemed even sharper than before, and his face had grown ashen. There was a hint of bestial ferociousness in his glaring, feverish eyes, which was enough to make one think that he had been experiencing a degree of mental strain.

'What he said is true,' said Nitcho, his voice hoarse and rasping. He then licked his lips like an animal. 'There was no leg. I made it up.'

As the three police officers exchanged glances, it was as though a dam had been broken and a torrent of words now gushed forth. The story Nitcho told turned the case on its head.

It all began late in the afternoon on the 28th of February...

Nitcho said that he had gone to collect firewood in the woodland at the rear of the temple, and that he had heard a sound, as though someone were digging in the garden of the Black Cat, right at the bottom of the bank. He peered down innocently and saw that it was Daigo Itojima. When

Nitcho asked what he was digging the hole for, the owner replied that he was burying the cat because it had died.

However, two or three days later, when Nitcho returned to the same spot to collect some more firewood, he heard a cat meowing in the garden. Recalling what he'd seen the other night, the monk shuddered, and, when he looked down from the top of the bank, he saw the black cat, which should have been dead, peering back at him from under the *engawa*, its eyes aglitter, and meowing incessantly.

Nitcho was startled by this, but he was not so superstitious as to think that it was the ghost of a cat.

If the cat's alive, then Mr Itojima must have been lying. But why would he lie about that? And, then, what's really buried over there?

Thinking this, Nitcho glanced over at the hole he had seen Daigo digging, and once again his heart skipped a beat. Leaves had not yet covered the garden, and he could see that the upturned earth covered quite a sizeable area. While it was impossible to tell what had been buried there, it was clearly something big. Although unable to pinpoint the reason for it, the monk felt a vague sense of unease. As he looked down from the top of the bank, however, he suddenly became aware of somebody's gaze burning into him. He quickly looked around, and all of a sudden his eyes met another pair staring back at him from the gap between the sliding doors in the rear room of the Black Cat. These eyes immediately vanished behind the sliding door, but Nitcho felt an increasingly strong sense of fore-boding. The eyes were all he could see, so he couldn't tell who it was, but he was certain that they belonged to a woman. In which case, other than Mrs Itojima's, they could be only Kayoko's, Tamae's or O-Kimi's, but he still had the feeling that the eyes he had seen had belonged to none of them.

The next day, Nitcho remembered that he had not col-lected the previous month's rent from the Black Cat, so, while he was there, he enquired off-handedly about the woman in the sitting room at the back. The three girls work-ing there said that it had to be Mrs Itojima. When he asked whether it could have been anybody apart from her, the girls told him that it was impossible, that O-Shige had had an allergic reaction and would not even let them see her. 'Why do you ask, Nitcho-san?' 'Yes, why are you so inter-ested?' 'Oh, I get it, it's because Nitcho-san is sweet on Mrs Itojima!' 'He's in love with her!' 'Oh, look! He's blushing!'...

As the girls teased him, Nitcho fled back to the temple in embarrassment, but what he'd seen in the garden and the back room continued to weigh on his mind, and so he sneaked back to the grove of trees. And, when he looked down from the bank, he saw that the hole had been neatly covered with fallen leaves. The monk's anxiety grew more intense. His sense of curiosity ignited. To alleviate his anxi-ety, he had no choice but to ascertain whether the woman in that back room was indeed Mrs Itojima. And this only fanned his curiosity further. Nitcho decided to keep watch over the room from the top of the bank. Lying down in the grass there, he had a perfect view of the tatami room below. Not only were the sliding doors always tightly closed these days, but the glass in them had been carefully covered with paper so that it was impossible to see inside. *Even so*, thought Nitcho, *whoever that woman may be, she's still human. She'll have to heed the call of nature several times a day.* The toilet was at the end of the *engawa*, on the other side of the sliding doors. And so, Nitcho waited, with all the patience of a cat stalking a mouse…

'So, did you see who it was in the end?' the station chief cut in, having had his fill of Nitcho's loquaciousness.

The monk's eyes flashed.

'Oh, I saw her all right.'

'You did? Who was it then? Mrs Itojima?'

'No, it wasn't Mrs Itojima. It was a girl I didn't recognize. Somebody I'd never seen before.'

This revelation was like music to Murai's ears, but it sent the station chief and the chief inspector into a panic.

'But then… surely she must have been a nurse or something, and Mrs Itojima was still in the room…'

'No, Chief Inspector,' Nitcho said flatly. 'I'm afraid that's quite impossible.'

There was a venomous quality to his voice.

'She was undoubtedly the only person in the room,' he continued. 'And what's more, she was wearing Mrs Itojima's kimono. By which I mean to say that she had disguised herself as Mrs Itojima and was fooling everybody in the process.'

At this point, the monk launched into another soliloquy.

Shortly after that, he said, he heard that Mr Itojima was selling up and moving away. Time was of the essence. On the last day, he happened upon the two women who had been fired in the street and tried to ascertain whether either of them had in fact seen Mrs Itojima's face since that night. Neither of them had.

It was around that time, however, that an article appeared in the newspaper about a number of bodies that had been dug up under the *engawa* of an empty house, causing quite a stir. Unable to bear it any longer, Nitcho decided that he had to find an answer to this terrible mystery. Otherwise, he would not be able to sleep at night.

'That's why I went digging.'

After Nitcho finished talking, he was detained by the police for several hours, during which time he was surrounded by detectives who rained down all manner of questions on him. At first, he repeated everything he had told the three officers without hesitation, his eyes flashing like a wild beast, but then, later, he suddenly collapsed and began foaming at the mouth. He had had an attack of some chronic illness.

'What on earth is going on here?!' the station chief exclaimed, looking a little dazed and exhausted from all the excitement of the morning. 'Are you telling me that it wasn't Ayuko who was killed, but Mrs Itojima? And that Ayuko had been masquerading as Mrs Itojima for two whole weeks?'

The chief inspector sat there in silence, stroking his chin. Instead, it was Murai who spoke up rather tentatively.

'I've actually been thinking that for some time, Chief. It's a little suspicious that people who live and work in the same house wouldn't see a person for as long as a fortnight just because she had a few pimples on her face. I think something sinister was going on…'

'But why would Ayuko have to pretend to be Mrs Itojima? Wouldn't that be an exceedingly dangerous thing to do?'

'It would indeed, sir. But with "Mrs Itojima" in the back room, nobody suspected her husband, even though he sold off the bar. Imagine how it would have been if his wife had suddenly disappeared, and he tried to sell up. What would people—or those three women, at least—think? That he needed money to run away. That's why he had to make out that his wife was still alive until he got his hands on the money.'

'Hmm…'

The station chief stroked his chin, while the chief inspector scratched his head.

'I believe this also explains why the black cat was killed,' Murai continued. 'Mrs Itojima must have doted on that cat. Having witnessed the murder, it would have been wary of Mr Itojima, so he must have killed it and buried them

81

together. But, realizing that the girls working there would get suspicious if the cat disappeared, he acquired a replacement and pretended that it was the same cat. The cats are brothers from the same litter, and we know that Daigo went to pick up the other one from its previous owner on the evening of the 28th. So, it can't have been Ayuko who was killed. Rather, Ayuko and Daigo must have killed O-Shige.'

The station chief groaned. But then a thought seemed to strike him. 'Of course... Why didn't I think of that before? Didn't Constable Hasegawa say that he saw the Itojimas passing by his police box on the night of the 14th?'

However, it soon became clear that Hasegawa had not in fact got a clear view of the woman's face. She had been wearing a shawl that covered the tip of her nose, and, as she passed by, she had kept her head down and her body pressed into Daigo's. Given the circumstances, it was not at all unreasonable for Hasegawa to have assumed that it was O-Shige. And so, all doubts regarding what Nitcho had said were dispelled. It was not Ayuko but O-Shige who had been murdered, thus making Ayuko instead the culprit.

The case had been turned on its head, and a nationwide search was launched for Daigo Itojima and his mistress, Ayuko.

The news made the headlines of the evening edition of the papers that same day, but there were two people who were especially surprised, or rather, who took a special interest in it.

Shunroku Kazama read the news in his office and rubbed his eyes in disbelief. Like a lion in a cage, he began pacing back and forth about the room, then finally stormed out, his face like thunder. Soon enough, he found himself in Omori, at a splendid traditional-style restaurant and inn called the Matsuzuki. This establishment had been built by Kazama himself, and he used it as a place to entertain clients and to meet his various mistresses.

'Oh, it's you, sir! Hello,' the hostess exclaimed, rushing from the back while Kazama was undoing his shoelaces in the gleaming vestibule.

'Ah, O-Chika! Hello. I'm here to see…'

'Yes, sir. The mistress is taking a bath at the moment.'

'Not O-Setsu!'

'Oh, you're here to see this new flame of yours, then? What a wicked man you are, Mr Kazama! Giving up the mistress just like that! It would be one thing, you know, if this new flame were a woman, but… Ha-ha! You're blushing, I can see! Yes, yes, he's here. He hasn't run off anywhere, don't you worry.'

Kazama gave a wry smile.

'I imagine he's still sleeping?'

'On the contrary! He was reading the evening paper when, all of a sudden, he got into a terrible state and demanded that I bring in all the papers from the last few days. He was very insistent!'

'Newspapers?'

83

Kazama's eyes glittered with relief, and he went striding off into the depths of the inn. Having heard his voice, a woman came rushing out of the bathroom and called to him, but, without even turning around, he just carried on down the corridor, making his way towards the annexe at the back.

'Are you in there, K?' he called out.

Without waiting for an answer, however, he threw open the sliding door to reveal a tasteful room and there, sitting in the middle of it, surrounded by newspapers, none other than Kosuke Kindaichi.

'K-K-Kazama!' Kindaichi stammered, seeing the construction boss's face. 'Th-th-this case… it's a "f-f-faceless corpse" case, isn't it? The v-victim and the c-culprit—they were the other way around! I'm sure that o-o-old Y—— in Okayama will be pleased to hear this!'

As he spoke, he scratched his shaggy hair, laughing like a lunatic all the while.

CHAPTER SEVEN

It was the evening of the 29th of March, three days after the case was turned on its head.

A strange man turned up at the police station where the case was being investigated. In one of the rooms, a group of senior officers had gathered to hold a briefing, when in came one of the office boys and handed a business card to the station chief. Looking at it, the station chief saw that the card belonged to one of the senior officers of the Tokyo Metropolitan Police, and that it carried a note scrawled in pen:

> *I hereby introduce Kosuke Kindaichi. I would be grateful if you would accept his assistance in the Black Cat Cafe murder case. Regards, etc.*

The station chief frowned.

'Is this man here?'

'Yes, sir. He's waiting at reception.'

'Very well. Send him through.'

The station chief took another look at the business card, before sliding it across the desk to the chief inspector.

'Have you ever heard of this chap?'

The chief inspector looked quizzically at the writing on the card and shook his head. He then handed the card to Detective Murai, but the latter knew nothing about it, either.

'Maybe he has some evidence for us.'

'Yes, maybe.'

Even so, the station chief was nervous, given the rank of the man whose name appeared on the business card. There was also that vague line about 'assistance', which set Murai wondering what kind of person this man was. When Kindaichi walked in, however, Murai couldn't believe his eyes.

'Why, it's you!'

Kosuke Kindaichi was dressed, as always, in a threadbare kimono and a pair of *hakama*. As he entered the room, he gave a quick bow of the head to nobody in particular, but when he spotted Murai, he chuckled and said, 'Oh, hello! From yesterday, yes?'

There was a mischievous glint in his eye.

'Do you know this man, Detective?' the station chief asked doubtfully, turning to Murai.

'You could say that, sir…'

Murai sighed as he glared warily at Kosuke Kindaichi. It transpired that, after the recent revelations had come to light, the detective had thought it was necessary to start the investigation over, so he had revisited all the people connected with the case, in order to interview them anew. No matter where he went, however, he had encountered this man. At first, he thought little of it, but after it happened a few times, the detective began to grow suspicious. Then, when he found him yet again at O-Kimi's aunt's home, he asked the man what on earth he was up to.

'Me?' the man had said, laughing. 'I'm looking for a phantom.'

Then, leaving the detective speechless, the man had sauntered off without saying another word.

Later, Murai asked O-Kimi who he was.

'I don't really know,' she said. 'But he said he was an acquaintance of Mr Kazama's. You know, the gentleman who was Mrs Itojima's lover.'

Murai's pulse quickened when he heard this. Kazama was a prominent figure in the case, after all. Could this man be a suspect? His suspicions thus alerted, Murai decided to follow him.

Whether he was aware of this or not, the man headed from Meguro to Shibuya and then took a train as far as G—— Town, where he proceeded to the Back Cut. By now, Murai was growing more and more suspicious, but his quarry was perfectly composed. He walked at a leisurely pace, carrying a rattan cane, and wore his hat pushed back on his head. He even seemed to be whistling. When he reached the back of the Renge-in, however, the rhythm of his footsteps changed. Just as Murai began to wonder what was going on, the man suddenly vanished.

Startled by this, Murai ran over in a panic to where the man had only just been. There, he found a mud wall that had begun to crumble, creating a hole just big enough for a person to pass through. How the man had vanished was clear, but the reason for it was not. All this only strengthened Murai's suspicions, and so he followed him through the wall.

There was, as has already been observed, a coppice of trees there, a remnant of old Musashino. It was early spring, but the yellow leaves on the ground still lent the place a look of desolation. Murai looked around, but he was unable to spot the man. He then listened carefully but could not hear any footsteps. The detective felt a little uneasy, but, having come this far, he could not just give up now. Picking his way through the withered grass, he gradually plunged deeper into the coppice. Suddenly he caught sight of the man up ahead. He was standing against a large zelkova tree, staring off into the distance. He looked awfully tense.

Murai craned his neck, trying to see what the man was looking at, but he was too far away to make it out. He took a step forward, but he was still too far. Then he took a second, and a third and a fourth step, and all of a sudden he lost his balance. The trees went spinning before his eyes, and, before he knew it, he found himself falling into a hole and making a terrific thud.

As the detective found out later, it was an air-raid shelter that had been dug during the war. Fortunately, there was a deep layer of fallen leaves at the bottom, so he was not injured, but for a few moments, he lay there, stunned, and did not know where he was. As he sat up and looked around himself, the man he had been following appeared from above, looking down at him and laughing.

'Oh, Detective!' he said. 'I hope you're not seeing stars!'

And with that, the man sauntered off. That is to say, the same man who was now standing before Murai at the station.

The detective heaved a deep sigh.

The station chief looked at the two men sceptically.

'Kosuke Kindaichi, I presume?' he said.

'At your service.'

'Please, take a seat. This is a friend of yours?' he said, indicating the business card.

'Something like that, yes.'

'Well, what can we do for you?'

'It's really a question of what I can do for you, sir. As I told the detective only yesterday, I'd very much like to show you a phantom.'

'A phantom?'

The station chief and chief inspector looked at each other in confusion. The latter was about to say something, when the station chief cut him off with a look.

'What exactly do you mean by "a phantom"?' he asked.

'Exactly that, gentlemen... There may well be lots of phantoms around after the war nowadays, but the one I'm about to show you is the culprit in the murder case at the Black Cat.'

Having given his colleague another baffled look, the station chief leant slightly across the table.

'Are you saying you know where we can find Daigo Itojima and Ayuko Kuwano?'

'I am, indeed.'

Kosuke Kindaichi feigned nonchalance about this, but, hearing these three little words, the other men in the room jumped up in their chairs, as though he had just set off a bomb.

The station chief just stared at the man in disbelief. Was the man stupid, crazy or somebody truly exceptional?

'Well, where on earth are they? Where are they hiding?'

'All will be revealed momentarily. But before that, I have a little request to make.'

'And what is that?'

'Would you mind sending for Nitcho again? There's something I'd like to ask him. And once I have the answer to that, I'll take you straight to Daigo and Ayuko.'

For several moments, the station chief just stared at Kosuke Kindaichi, wondering what to do. But then, all of a sudden, he looked down at the business card he was fingering, before he turned to the chief inspector with a decisive look.

'Get on the telephone to the police box in G—— Town. Have Hasegawa bring Nitcho here as soon as possible.'

'Oh, and, if you wouldn't mind,' Kosuke Kindaichi added, 'tell him while you're at it that, if he does find Nitcho, he should telephone the station first and let us know.'

Once the chief inspector had finished making the call, he turned to Kosuke Kindaichi.

'Kindaichi-san,' he said, 'you mentioned something about a phantom a little earlier... Do you mean to suggest that Ayuko is dead?'

Kosuke Kindaichi raised his eyebrows.

'Ayuko? Why ever would you think that? Is the girl dead? No, the phantom I have in mind is somebody who's supposed to be dead but is, in fact, very much alive.'

The chief inspector was at a loss for words. Even after hearing Nitcho's testimony, he was still unable to abandon the theory that it was Ayuko who had been killed, and that O-Shige was the one who killed her.

Having been keeping a wary eye on Kosuke Kindaichi all this time, Murai was the next to speak up.

'I've only just remembered this, Kindaichi-san, but aren't you an acquaintance of Mr Kazama's?'

Hearing this, Kosuke Kindaichi grinned.

'And how exactly did you come by that piece of information, Detective?' He laughed. 'Ah, of course! You must have heard it from O-Kimi.'

'Perhaps. Perhaps not. Regardless of that, would you mind telling us what exactly the nature of your acquaintance with Mr Kazama is?'

'We were at high school together.'

Kosuke Kindaichi then launched into a seemingly unstoppable monologue.

'The school was in Tohoku, you see. When we left school, it was just the two of us—him and me. We came to Tokyo together. Then, after a while, he found lodgings in a boarding house in Kanda, where he idled away his days, while I set sail for America. He stayed in Japan, and what became of him? He became a delinquent. He was a tough guy, a loan-shark, a blackmailer. Later, after I returned from America, this delinquent had turned over a new leaf. He'd joined a crime syndicate and risen up the ranks. We'd still see each other from time to time, but it was at that point that I was drafted into the army, and we lost touch again. I didn't see him again for a good six or seven years. But then I was demobbed last year, and, just after that happened, I had a little business to attend to in the Seto Inland Sea, and it was on the train journey back that it all happened. You see, a gang of black-marketeers came barging in and, my goodness, they were so brazen that they were just impossible to deal with. They were a real menace and caused nothing but trouble for us good, honest passengers. But nobody dared to say a word against them. We were all shaking in our boots, myself included. After a while, they grew more and more emboldened, but when their shenanigans reached a point that was simply intolerable, one man stood up. He grabbed the man who appeared to be the leader of the gang and said something to him. Shocked and gladdened by this in equal measure, we were all bracing ourselves for some terrible scene to ensue, but then something unexpected happened. No sooner had he whispered something in the boss's ear than the entire situation changed. The group of menacing thugs suddenly stopped what they were doing and fell silent. In fact, not only did they fall silent, but they also bowed down before the man, showing extreme deference and respect. Everybody there gathered around the hero, thanking him profusely. Some of the ladies looked a little dazed by it all. But then, I too was mightily impressed. What a great man he must be, I thought, to subdue these tyrants whom even the police did not dare to approach with only a few words. Then I took another look and finally the penny dropped. It was Kazama! I was so happy to see him, I can't tell you. Thinking this was the perfect opportunity to reveal myself to this people's hero, I tapped him on the shoulder and said, "Hey, haven't I seen you somewhere before?" He turned, took a good look at me and said, "Well I never! If it isn't old K!" Such was the scene of my reunion with Shunroku Kazama. When I told him that I had nowhere to go, his invitation to stay with him for a while came unhesitatingly—an offer I wasted no time in accepting.'

Stunned by this tale, the officers in the room just stared blankly at Kosuke Kindaichi, wondering who on earth this perfectly earnest-looking man in their midst was. Finally, stifling a guffaw, the station chief said, 'Yes, I see… So, you're staying at Mr Kazama's pleasure for the time being, are you?'

'Guilty as charged, I'm afraid. Well, strictly speaking, I'm not living with him. The house he's put me in is where he keeps his mistress. Or should that be mistresses? For a man who says he's "not particularly interested in women", he certainly has a lot of them… At any rate, he came bursting in to see me the other night. He was so worked up that I wondered what on earth was going on. He told me that he was mixed up in this case, but, since that fact hadn't been reported in the papers, I was unaware of it. Well, he told me that there were some things that just couldn't be explained in this case and asked whether I'd be willing to try my hand at solving the mystery. And the reason he asked me, you see, is that I used be in the detective business a long time ago…'

'Come again? What business did you say you were in?'

'The detective business. In short, I was a sort of private detective.'

The station chief let out a short cry of astonishment before hurriedly turning his attention back to the business card.

'You said you were recently in the Seto Inland Sea,' he said. 'By that, you wouldn't happen to mean Gokumon Island, would you?'

'The very same! You heard about the case, then?'

'I did, indeed. It even made the papers here in Tokyo. What an odd case that was! Well, then, Mr...'

Deeply impressed, the station chief looked at Kindaichi anew. Meanwhile, the chief inspector and Murai seemed to be in shock; all of Murai's doubts had been dispelled in an instant.

'Kosuke Kindaichi, at your service, gentlemen!'

'So, that explains why you're on such good terms with this man,' said the station chief, examining the business card in his hand once more. Then, leaning across the table he added, 'Forgive me for saying so, Kindaichi-san, but you're not quite how I pictured you... Anyway, you've decided to help us with this case, is that correct?'

'That's right, sir. I do owe Mr Kazama a favour or two, after all. I may not care much for the yakuza and their ways, but this case piqued my interest right from the very start. After all, it's not every day that you come across a "faceless corpse" case. They can be quite a challenge! That's why it took me until yesterday to solve the puzzle.'

Startled by this unexpected revelation, the station chief stared at Kosuke Kindaichi, frowning.

'Puzzle, you say? Is there a puzzle in this case?'

'Oh, yes, sir! There most certainly is. And what's more, it's a most ingenious one. Although, please don't misunderstand me: in saying this, I'm not trying to boast about having solved the puzzle before you. You see, I managed to obtain some very important information that you don't know about…' Kosuke Kindaichi turned to Detective Murai. 'Mr Kazama asked me to apologize to you on his behalf, Detective. When you went to see him the other day, there was something he didn't tell you.'

'Oh, and what's that?' said Murai, leaning forward.

'Well, it has to do with Mr Itojima. When he first went to see Mr Kazama, the owner of the Black Cat tried to intimidate him…'

'Oh, I knew all about that.'

'Yes, but that's neither here nor there. What you don't know is that, in his excitement, Mr Itojima let something slip. That the reason O-Shige had left Japan was because she'd poisoned her previous husband in Tokyo. Quite a remarkable woman, you'll agree.'

Everybody in the room was taken aback.

'So, O-Shige was a past offender?' the station chief said, trying to catch his breath.

'Yes, but it seems that she was never brought to trial. She managed to escape to China before that could happen. By rights, Mr Kazama ought to have told the detective here, but he held back because he wasn't sure whether it was really true or not. Because he told this to me, however, I was able to conduct a little investigation of my own and find out a thing or two about O-Shige's past life.'

'And what did you find out?'

'Well, without any witnesses, it's difficult to be certain, but I'm confident in my findings. There is something else, however, that supports my conclusion, and that's something that O-Shige let slip to Mr Kazama. Apparently, she once mentioned that she suffered a lot because, just after she arrived in Manchuria, the China Incident happened. So, if she'd committed a crime in Japan and run away, it would have to have taken place in the first half of 1937. So, I went to the newspaper company and scoured through all the papers from that time. And this is what I found...'

Kosuke Kindaichi extracted a photograph from the notebook he was carrying in the breast of his kimono. Taking the photo, the station chief saw that it showed a girl of seventeen or eighteen in pigtails, dressed in a plain silk kimono. She was certainly pretty, but not remarkably so; if anything, one would have described her as an ordinary-looking young woman.

'Who is this?'

'I borrowed this photo from the newspaper's archive. There was a note attached to it. Listen while I read it to you. "Hanako Matsuda, 17, eldest daughter of Fukugawa carpenter Yonezo Matsuda. After leaving primary school, worked as a waitress at the Silver Moon cafe in Tokyo's

Ginza district, where she was spotted by the Western-style painter Junpei Miake, who married her. The Miake house was a wealthy one, but, because of differences in background, the mistress, Yasuko, did not get on with her new daughter-in-law, leading to constant arguments at home. On 3 June 1937, Hanako attempted to poison her mother-in-law, but ended up killing her husband, Junpei, instead, after which she fled. Since then, her whereabouts have been unknown. There are rumours that she committed suicide. This photograph was taken in March 1936, when Hanako was still working at the Silver Moon."'

As Kosuke Kindaichi read on, the station chief grew more and more excited. By the time he had finished reading, the chief was breathing heavily in excitement.

'I remember that case, too,' he said. 'I was at the station in Kagurazaka at the time, and the Miake house was next door in Ushigome-Yarai. So, are you saying that in her previous life O-Shige Daigo was, in fact, Hanako Matsuda?'

'Precisely. I checked all the newspapers from the first half of 1937, and then, just to be sure, all the papers from the year before, but there was no other case of a woman having killed her husband and then disappearing. Hanako Matsuda was the only one. And then there's the fact that their ages match. So, I showed the photograph first to Kazama, then to O-Kimi, Kayoko and Tamae.'

'And? They all said it was O-Shige?'

'None of them could say for sure. Any woman would change a lot over the course of a decade. Moreover, a woman in her position would have been conscious of this and gone to great lengths to alter her old appearance, so it is little wonder that the four of them could not immediately say that it was her. But then, neither could they say that it *wasn't* her…'

For several moments, everybody in the room fell silent. It was as if some terrible darkness had swept through the room like a rising tide.

When the station chief realized that his fists were clenched and palms were sweating, he took out a handkerchief and began to dry them.

'In that case…' he began to speak. But just then, the telephone on the desk began to ring. He picked up the receiver immediately. 'Hello? Ah. Yes. We'll be expecting you.'

Putting the receiver down, he turned again to Kosuke Kindaichi.

'That was Hasegawa. He and Nitcho will be here presently.'

Much to everyone's surprise, however, Kosuke Kindaichi jumped up when he heard this. He replaced the photograph in his notebook and put on his hat.

'In th-th-that case,' he stammered, 'we must go at once.'

Taken aback by this, the station chief and the chief inspector looked at Kosuke Kindaichi in astonishment. Murai jumped to his feet, looking tense. In that instant, it seemed that only he had fathomed Kosuke Kindaichi's plan.

'Quickly, gentlemen, there's no time to lose. We must get to Daigo and Ayuko. We can deal with Nitcho later. Chief, make sure that when Nitcho arrives, he's kept here. Tell the duty officer that under no circumstances is he to be let out of this police station. Now, gentlemen, let's go.'

The two senior officers nervously got to their feet. Although they had no idea what was going on, one thing was clear: that this man was going to lead them to the bizarre finale of this case.

Murai was already making for the door.

CHAPTER EIGHT

While all this was going on, Tamekichi and two other workmen were burning copper scraps and wood chippings in a bonfire in the back garden of the Black Cat Cafe. After the recent discovery there, renovation work on the building had been halted temporarily, but now the police had given permission for the work to be resumed. And so, there was nothing untoward about the men's presence there, but still, they were strangely quiet. Not only that, but the fact that they kept pricking their ears up at the sound of footsteps outside and looking at their wristwatches suggested that they were waiting for somebody. What was even more bizarre was that they appeared to have brought with them shovels and pickaxes, which they had laid in one corner of the garden. After all, why would they need shovels and pickaxes for a simple renovation job?

'They're coming!' Tamekichi suddenly whispered. 'I think I can hear footsteps.'

A tension suddenly gripped the three men, who then dispersed from around the bonfire.

The station chief and chief inspector, who had entered through the rear gate of the Black Cat, raised their eyebrows in surprise when they saw the workmen there. Murai, on the other hand, looked at Kosuke Kindaichi's face searchingly.

'These men are going to do a little job for me,' Kosuke Kindaichi said, grinning. 'Only they could bring in shovels and pickaxes without raising any suspicions. The police would have noticed it, otherwise. Well, shall we get to it, gentlemen? I'd hate to keep you waiting any longer.'

Taking the lead, Kosuke Kindaichi then set off to climb the steep bank at the back of the garden. Following him, Tamekichi and the other labourers each took either a shovel or a pickaxe and started up the steep incline. Then Murai and finally the station chief and the chief inspector followed behind them. They all did this in perfect silence: not one asked where they were going or why. But, judging by the tools the workmen were carrying, they all expected some terrible truth to be revealed, and, while this heavy silence weighed on them, they could hear their hearts pounding.

Reaching the top of the bank, they found themselves in a coppice.

'Please be careful,' Kosuke Kindaichi said, turning around. 'There are air-raid shelters dug all over the place. Why, only yesterday, the poor detective…'

But when he saw Detective Murai's sullen expression, he laughed and his words trailed off.

After passing through the coppice, they came to a grave-yard packed with tombstones of all shapes and sizes. Yet, the times being what they were, it looked as if few people now came to visit these graves. No doubt, since the war, there would be fewer relatives around to tend to them, and so the entire place was crumbling and neglected.

The spot to which Kosuke Kindaichi led them was at the far side, and it was so overgrown that it was impossible to tell whether it was still the graveyard or the coppice. There they saw a single tombstone, so worn that it was now illegible, lying on its side, surrounded by a thick layer of fallen leaves.

'Would you mind clearing away the leaves, Tamekichi?'

The workman wielded his shovel and did as Kosuke Kindaichi had asked, revealing a layer of recently upturned yellow soil. The two senior police officers gulped when they saw this.

'The manner in which the upturned earth has been covered up with fallen leaves is the same technique that was used in the garden of the Black Cat,' said Kosuke Kindaichi. 'So, would you mind removing the tombstone and digging there for me?'

The stone was small and not terribly heavy, so this was soon accomplished. There were a lot of leaves that had been caught under the stone itself.

'Please take note,' Kosuke Kindaichi continued. 'The culprit was in quite a hurry. It was a real blunder to replace the gravestone *after* spreading the leaves. Thanks to this, it didn't take me long to find the right grave.'

Once the leaves had been cleared away, Murai pitched in, helping to dig. It was clear that the soil had been upturned recently, since it was soft enough to dig with one's hands.

'You must be as quiet as possible, gentlemen,' Kosuke Kindaichi said. 'And please try not to be too rough. I'd hate for you to damage it. I think that's enough of the pickaxe now.'

Tamekichi and one of the other workmen dug using shovels. The other workman set his pickaxe aside and began to dig with his bare hands. Having relinquished his pickaxe, Murai, unable to stand idly by, also began digging with his hands, while the other three men watched on, unable to tear their eyes away from the scene before them. Perspiring, the two senior officers took off their caps periodically to mop their brow. Meanwhile, Kosuke Kindaichi kept nervously taking off and replacing his hat again.

By now, the hole in the ground was rather deep. Suddenly, one of the labourers, who had stuck his hand in the soil, cried out and recoiled.

'What is it?' Kosuke Kindaichi asked, his breathing quick.

'Whatever it is, it's soft... and cold...'

'Very well,' said Kosuke Kindaichi, looking around at all the other men. 'Gentlemen, I should caution you in advance, lest there be any unwanted cries of surprise. As you have all probably guessed, I expect we shall find a body buried here. Now, please, carry on digging.'

The labourers exchanged a few uncertain glances with one another, but their curiosity seemingly outweighed their fear. They threw down their shovels and began to excavate the dirt with their bare hands. Soon, some ashen skin appeared. To their surprise, this body, too, was without a stitch of clothing on it. It appeared to be buried face down, and little by little the back was revealed.

'Damn it! The body has been stripped so that it can't be identified by the clothing. We're lucky that we found it when we did. Another week and it would have been another "faceless corpse".'

'Say!' the chief inspector exclaimed. 'This one looks like it's a man, doesn't it?'

Judging by the build and the skin tone, it was definitely a man. This seemed to come as a surprise to the station chief as well, who, grim-faced, looked to Kosuke Kindaichi for some explanation.

'Why yes, of course it's a man, Chief Inspector! What else were you expecting?'

'Well… I thought that it might be… Ayuko?'

'Ayuko? You must be joking. That devil can't die. I've been telling you all along that she's alive… Ah!'

Even Kosuke Kindaichi cried out in fright when he saw the back of the head that had finally been exposed. The others all gasped and turned pale. Cold sweat seemed to seep from every pore of their bodies. To everybody's horror, the back of the head was split open like a pomegranate.

Kosuke Kindaichi extracted a handkerchief from the sleeve of his kimono and nervously mopped the perspiration from his face.

'I hope the face is still intact… Detective Murai, I'm sorry to have to ask this, but would you mind lifting the body up and showing the face to Tamekichi here? I believe he will recognize the man.'

'Here, you'd better use these,' said the station chief, throwing him a pair of leather gloves.

Having put them on, Murai placed his hands on the shoulders of the body and heaved it up. The face of the corpse was covered in soil. The chief inspector then took out a handkerchief and, hand trembling, proceeded to wipe away the dirt.

'Take a look, Tamekichi. Don't be afraid. You're in charge here. Be brave and tell us who it is.'

The face of the corpse was horribly contorted, but it was not as deformed as Kosuke Kindaichi feared it might be, and the degree of decomposition was not so bad.

Tamekichi gritted his teeth and took a good look at that terrible countenance.

'Argh! It's… it's… it's the owner of the Black Cat!'

Kosuke Kindaichi turned to the station chief and the chief inspector, but since it was already known that the body was a man's, the news came as no great shock, and so the two of them did not look all that surprised. The station chief turned to the private detective.

'Mr Itojima's been killed as well, then?' he said, nodding. 'Damn it! And to think we wasted all that time and energy looking for him. When was he murdered?'

'On the evening of the 14th. After passing by the police box in G—— Town, he was lured into the temple grounds and dealt a sharp blow to the head, which finished him off. All that remained was to hide the body. Meanwhile, the police were hunting for him as the man responsible for O-Shige's murder, or at least an accomplice to it. That was the real culprit's plan all along.'

'And by the real culprit, you mean Ayuko?'

'Precisely.'

'So where is Ayuko now?' the chief inspector cut in.

'She's in this very temple. In the storehouse over there…'

The sun was already beginning to set. The enormous, deserted temple grounds were beginning to fade into a grey light, and the cold wind was beginning to make itself felt. The men directed their gaze to where Kosuke Kindaichi was pointing and saw a solitary earthen storehouse in the far reaches of the grounds, set far back from the main hall and the temple kitchens, near a small shrine that was known as the inner sanctuary. The storehouse had been constructed to house various fixtures and treasures of the temple and appeared to have been built at a remove from the other buildings for fear of fire.

For a moment, everybody was silent, but then, all of a sudden, Murai broke into a run. The station chief and chief inspector followed after him.

'Tamekichi,' said Kosuke Kindaichi, turning to the labourer, 'would you please bring a pickaxe with you. You two others, stay here, please.'

Tamekichi did as he was bidden and followed the private detective.

The door to the storehouse was secured from the outside with an enormous lock.

'I believe that Nitcho is in possession of the key to this lock. There may be others, but it seems a pity to wake poor Nissho. So, let's break it open with the pickaxe.'

The lock was soon broken. Kosuke Kindaichi thanked Tamekichi for all that he'd done and dismissed him. He then placed his hand to the door. Was it nerves that had made his palms clammy with perspiration?

'Please be careful, everyone. It's like hunting for a wounded animal. You mustn't let your guard down just because it's a woman.'

The policemen thus warned, Kosuke Kindaichi took a deep breath and pushed open the heavy door with all his might.

'Look out!' cried Murai, pushing the private detective out of harm's way.

Caught off guard, Kosuke Kindaichi went tumbling to the ground just as the gunshot rang out and a bullet went whistling past his head. Even the private detective had not anticipated that their quarry would be carrying a gun. Were it not for Murai, he would have been killed instantly with a bullet to the head.

'Don't move, or I'll shoot!' came a high-pitched woman's voice from somewhere inside.

Still on the ground, Kosuke Kindaichi peered into the cavernous storehouse, and there, against the pitch-dark background, he saw a woman with short, bobbed hair standing in garish Western-style clothes. Despite being caked in make-up, her face was grim and ashen, and her eyes bulged with a crazed ferocity and a look of murderous intent. The muzzle of the pistol she was gripping was aimed squarely at Kosuke Kindaichi.

The policemen, never mind the private detective, all blanched in terror.

'Who the hell are you?' asked the woman, her voice trembling with uncontrollable rage and twisted by loathing and bitterness. 'You don't look like a policeman. But even so, what possible grudge could you have against me that you'd go so far as to drag me from the darkness out into the light?!' The words came from the very back of her throat, her voice strained by hysteria. 'Don't think I don't know what you've done! I saw you prowling around the cemetery just yesterday. I thought you were bad news and wanted to leave, but that idiot Nitcho wouldn't listen and refused to let me go. If it weren't for that bastard, I'd have run away a long time ago.' The woman was gritting and grinding her teeth so much that the men could hear it, but then suddenly, as though having lost her senses entirely, she began to shake her head from side to side. 'There's no point in telling you all this, though. It's all over for me. I've made up my mind! But as for you with the shaggy hair—I'm taking you with me! I'm not going to die alone. You and I are going to cross the Sanzu River hand in hand!'

'Enough!' the station chief shouted, stepping forward.

But Kosuke Kindaichi raised a hand and stopped him, shaking his head with a mournful look on his face. The woman brandished the pistol, preventing the chief from advancing any further.

'Now, get up!' the woman shouted.

Kosuke Kindaichi staggered to his feet and faced the woman square on. He no longer had the strength to think or the will to attempt anything. It was as if all his vitality had drained from his body, and now even just standing there took all his effort.

The three police officers were huddling together in a mad panic a little distance away, but there was nothing they could do. Their least movement would only hasten Kosuke Kindaichi's death. The pistol aimed at his chest was ready to fire at any moment.

The private detective felt a sense of languor creep up his entire body. If she was going to shoot, he would have preferred her not to drag this out.

The woman merely laughed in a way that no longer sounded human. She fixed her aim and placed her finger to the trigger.

Just then, however, she glanced over Kosuke Kindaichi's shoulder. The moment she saw the group of police officers standing there looking back at her, her resolve wavered. A look of hesitation flashed across her face, before it crumpled into that of a child on the verge of tears.

'O-Shige!' a deep voice echoed from behind the group. 'Don't be a fool!'

The woman suddenly turned the pistol she was holding and aimed it at her own heart. There was a loud bang, and she went reeling to the ground amid a cloud of smoke. As she did, Kosuke Kindaichi also staggered, as if he had been struck by the same bullet, but a strong, sure hand came to his aid, holding him firmly.

'K! You've got to pull yourself together!'

The hand belonged, of course, to Shunroku Kazama.

The three policemen rushed over to the woman. As the woman was in the final spasms of death, the station chief looked over at Kazama with a puzzled expression on his face.

'You just called this woman O-Shige! But can this really be her?'

'Yes, it can,' said Kosuke Kindaichi. 'It's O-Shige all right.'

'But, Kindaichi-san! You said earlier that this was Ayuko...'

'So I did, Chief,' the private detective said helplessly, still in the arms of Shunroku Kazama.

'She was O-Shige, the owner of the Black Cat—and, at the same time, she was Ayuko Kuwano, the girl from the Sunshine Dance Hall. O-Shige was leading a double life. Or should I say, playing a "double role"...'

CHAPTER NINE

The following day, in a private room at the Matsuzuki, Kosuke Kindaichi found himself surrounded by the station chief, the chief inspector and Detective Murai. Shunroku Kazama was also there, acting as host, and the men were attended by a rather seductive-looking woman, who was one of Kazama's many mistresses. By rights, the private detective ought to have gone to the police station to explain the case, but, after yesterday's excitement, he was so exhausted and his nerves were so overwrought that he lacked the strength to go anywhere. And so, concerned for his well-being, Kazama arranged for the police to come to him.

'I'm so pathetic,' said Kosuke Kindaichi, scratching his head in embarrassment. His face was pale, and his smile was feeble.

'It's only natural,' the station chief said sympathetically. 'Anybody who'd had a scrape with death would be feeling the same. It did get a little bit dicey back there, didn't it!'

'We were all in a state of shock,' the chief inspector said ruminatively.

'I dread to think what might have happened if Mr Kazama had arrived even a few seconds later,' Murai added, shuddering.

'You're not wrong there,' said Kosuke Kindaichi. 'She was in love with Kazama, that woman. That's why she looked so crestfallen when he shouted at her. Last night I couldn't get her face out of my head. She may have been bad news, but, when I think of that face, I can't help feeling sorry for her… So, what was the story there, Kazama? O-Setsu, cover your ears!'

'Don't talk rubbish!' Kazama retorted. 'Though I am glad to see that you're joking again. Last night you were in a delirium, and I was really quite worried. Wasn't I, O-Setsu?'

Sitting there with his heavy arms folded, Kazama turned to the woman beside him, who simply smiled in return. Then, as though spotting all of a sudden that the sake flask was empty, she got up and took it with her.

'If you need anything else, just ring the bell.'

'She's a good woman, O-Setsu,' Kosuke Kindaichi said as he watched her go. 'Haven't you had your fill of womanizing, Kazama? You ought to settle down with her.'

Kazama gave a wry smile.

'A man must have his liberties... Anyway, I've kept you gentlemen waiting long enough. I suppose we'd better get down to business.'

'Right,' said Kosuke Kindaichi, nodding vigorously. He took a sip of flat beer and then turned to the others present. 'It may seem like an odd place to begin, but there's a recurring theme in detective fiction known as the "faceless corpse" mystery. I heard about it from a friend in Okayama only recently, but it goes like this: person A wants to kill person B, but if person A does this, suspicion will immediately fall on him. In other words, it's widely known that A has a motive to kill B. So, what is A to do? Well, when A kills B, he disfigures the face, dresses the body in his own clothes, making it look as though it is he—that is, person A—who has been killed. After this, he goes into hiding, and the world thinks that B has killed A and then absconded, and so a search is launched for a person matching B's description. Therefore, A is safely assumed to be dead and can remain in hiding. Such is the trick. This recent case is very similar, but if you look at it more carefully, you will see that there is a fundamental difference. In the archetypal case, the main objective is to kill the person who could be used as a substitute—that is, person B—and that is why the crime is committed. Not so in the present case, however. O-Shige had no grudge against the woman who was killed. Her only aim was to kill her husband, Daigo Itojima. This is the crucial distinction between what happened here and the "faceless corpse" case in an ordinary detective novel, and that is why, the moment the motive was discovered, O-Shige had lost.'

The private detective took another sip of flat beer before continuing.

'I realized what the motive must be the moment I heard Kazama's suspicions about O-Shige's past. Then, when I discovered the case involving Hanako Matsuda in 1937, I could be sure at last. Hanako Matsuda tried to poison her mother-in-law, but ended up killing her husband, after which she fled to China. Naturally, she would have changed her name and kept her background under wraps. But some-how Daigo Itojima must have got wind of this and black-mailed her into marrying him. I'm certain that he'll have used O-Shige's good looks and body out there for his own nefarious purposes. There cannot have been any real love between a couple like that. Daigo may actually have been in love with the woman, but she can have harboured only loathing for him. Even so, she could not escape Daigo for fear that her secret would be revealed. It must have terri-fied her. And at the same time, the prospect of returning to Japan must have been horrifying. She had probably intended to live in the overseas territories for the rest of her life, but with the defeat she'd have had no choice but to be repatriated. This was an awful situation, but there was nothing she could do about it. And so, O-Shige hit upon an idea. Faced with the prospect of going back to this frightening country with this frightening man, she could at least get rid of one of them… And so, having given Daigo the slip, she made her way back to Japan on her own. No doubt she wanted to live as far away from Tokyo as possible, but, having been born and raised there, she just couldn't bring herself to do it in the end. Besides, ten long, hard years had passed, and each one of them had taken its toll on her face. The childish roundness of those former days was gone, and now she was rather long-faced. She was sure of these changes, but to accentuate them she decided to wear her hair in a completely different style and began dressing in traditional Japanese clothes. This is how she was when she was working at the cabaret in Yokohama, and how she was when Kazama met her there and took her as his mistress. There, she found a place where she could settle down, and, dare I say, fell in love with a man for the first time in her life. Having gained both stability in her life and satisfaction of her lust, she must have been drunk with happiness. But then Daigo turned up. The man she thought she had left behind forever appeared right before her very eyes. How furious O-Shige must have been in that moment. If it had only been a question of living, she might have given up. But now she was in love with a man called Kazama, and the attachment bound her to this life. This man had so cruelly ruined the happiness she had fought so hard to gain. O-Shige realized that there was no way she could ever be happy again, except by killing this man. That's right: the man, Daigo Itojima, who had come back to Japan and sought out O-Shige, was condemned to death the very moment he stood in front of her again.'

Nobody said a word. The station chief nodded in agreement with everything that Kosuke Kindaichi had said. Now that both Daigo and O-Shige were dead, it was impossible to verify all this, but everybody could only agree that what the private detective had deduced had to be close to the mark.

Kazama tried to pour his old friend some more beer, but the latter stopped him.

'No, I'm fine,' he said. 'It's better if I keep a clear head.'

He took another sip of the flat beer.

'So, let's go over the details of the case again from the very start. In the early hours of the 20th of this month, a woman's decomposing body was dug up in the back garden of the Black Cat. Investigations revealed that the body was that of a woman by the name of Ayuko Kuwano, that the murderer was the proprietress of the establishment, O-Shige, and that her husband, Daigo Itojima, was probably an accomplice. Kazama found out most of this from a telephone call he received from O-Kimi, and shortly after that he received a visit from Detective Murai, during which he learnt a few more details. At the time, however, Kazama was not surprised. Of course O-Shige was capable of something like this, he simply thought. But then, on the 26th, the case was suddenly turned on its head. It transpired that it was not Ayuko but O-Shige who had been killed, and that Ayuko, who had been thought the victim, was in fact the murderer. When he read the article, Kazama suddenly felt a sense of foreboding. Something, quite simply, didn't add up, something that he couldn't brush aside, and so he came to see me right away. He couldn't put his finger on it, but as I talked to him, I analysed his suspicion in the following way. The body was thought at first to be Ayuko's, but now it was said to be O-Shige's. So, the body could belong to either of them. So, was the body really Ayuko's? Kazama had his doubts. But I reasoned that it had to be Ayuko's. O-Shige had planned it so that we would think it was her body. That was my hypothesis. But why would O-Shige want to do that? That's where the secret of O-Shige's background came in handy. She wanted everybody to believe that she was dead. This was motive enough. It was also a much more plausible explanation for the identity of the suspicious woman who was hiding in the back room of the Black Cat. According to Detective Murai's theory, Ayuko was acting as a stand-in for O-Shige, but it would be very unnatural for somebody to have the nerve to carry on doing that for even a day or two, let alone two whole weeks, after having killed a man! Rather, it seemed more likely that O-Shige had one purpose in mind: namely, to plant the seed of doubt in the minds of the others by deliberately not showing her face. So yes, it had to be O-Shige, after all. Now, was there anything that would contradict this hypothesis? Indeed, there was. To be

119

more precise, Nitcho's testimony. However, because that will complicate things, let's leave that aside for now and proceed with the current hypothesis. So, we have Ayuko being the victim, and O-Shige as the murderer. And, of course, Daigo as an accomplice. Now, if we accept this, a problem arises. Why would they leave the bloodstains in the tatami room? Barely hidden as they were, it was only a matter of time before the new residents discovered them. The amount of blood was substantial, so even without a body, suspicions would be raised. Why would they just leave such vital evidence behind for anybody to find? All they had to do was tear off the panel of the sliding door that had been stained with blood, and they could have got rid of the tatami mat simply by taking it up and burning it. Given how easy it would have been, why not do it? Here, we must consider O-Shige's plan once more. She wanted to make it look as though she were dead or murdered, so she needed to leave behind as much evidence of a murder as possible. So, it makes sense that she would have left traces of blood in the room. But what about Daigo? O-Shige kills Ayuko. Daigo helps by burying the body. Then the two of them run away together. If that were really so, then would Daigo be willing to leave all that blood behind? Of course not. And what if Daigo knew about O-Shige's plan to use Ayuko's body as a substitute for her own? No, no, no. It's utterly unthinkable. He would never agree to such a plan. And even if he did, O-Shige might be safe, but suspicion would surely fall on him. It would be one thing to pretend that O-Shige was dead, but there's no way that he would agree to a plan that would implicate him as his wife's killer. In which case, it begins to look as if the whole thing was concocted by O-Shige alone without her husband's knowledge. That would certainly appear to be a more plausible explanation. But, if that were the case, the blood would be a problem. There was so much of it that Daigo couldn't have failed to notice it. What's more, the tatami mat had been swapped with the one that was originally under the chest of drawers, but to do this would have required moving the heavy chest—a task that O-Shige could never have managed on her own. So, we're left with the conclusion that Daigo must have helped. Only, what must he have made of the blood? When I reached this point in my deductions, I suddenly remembered the corpse of the black cat whose head had practically been severed...'

'Ah!' cried the three policemen, almost in unison.

'I see, I see!' said the station chief breathlessly. 'So, O-Shige fooled her husband into thinking that the blood was the cat's? That's why the black cat was killed?'

'Precisely!' said Kosuke Kindaichi, scratching his head in delight. 'You all believed that the black cat died because it had got caught up in the murder. But that would go against the very nature of cats. There's no animal in the world more difficult to kill than a cat. After all, don't they say that a cat has nine lives? And besides, judging by what had been done to it, I'd doubt that the cat was killed by chance. It certainly looked deliberate. The detective originally thought that the cat must have witnessed the murder of its owner and been spooked, hence the need to kill it. I, too, considered this at first, but really, that's like something out of a story by Edgar Allan Poe. And besides, even if it were true, the idea was troubling, since right from the start I didn't believe that O-Shige was the one who'd been murdered. But if we follow my hypothesis, then the killing of the cat fits perfectly. After committing a murder while her husband was out, O-Shige proceeded to kill the black cat. Then, when her husband came back, she could explain it away by saying that the cat had bitten or scratched her while she was playing with it and so she'd killed it in a fit of rage. She would have then shown him the blood-soaked body. O-Shige had always been given to hysteria, so Daigo would have been surprised but not so suspicious. And so, by killing the black cat, she was able to disguise the blood and conveniently, at the same time, make her husband dig a hole in the back garden to bury it. She was also able to pile on suspicion by sending him out to buy a replacement animal. She must have told him not to let on that she'd had a fit and killed the cat. After all, they wouldn't want people thinking that she was some kind of crazy she-devil, now would they? And it was a black cat, so nobody would be able to tell the difference, and they wouldn't have to mention it to anyone.'

'Hmm.' The station chief sighed heavily. 'I see. Well, that certainly explains Daigo's odd behaviour. So, without being any the wiser, he was dancing to her tune all along. And he had no idea that it was all a prelude to his own murder…'

'Exactly. That was the most cold-blooded, cruel and inhuman thing about this killer. Now, on the other hand, she applied greasepaint that was bad for her face deliberately to cause that unsightly reaction, so that she could retire to the tatami room at the back. We know that she'd had this same reaction last year, so she knew exactly which brand of greasepaint to apply. Even the fact that his wife closed the Black Cat on account of her bad reaction to the make-up didn't raise Daigo's suspicions. Then, out of the blue, she suggests to her husband that they sell the Black Cat and move away. Who knows what argument she used to get him to agree, but it was O-Shige's talents that kept the business afloat, after all, and so I dare say that Daigo would have had little choice but to go along with her idea…

'Now, let's change our focus a little and think about Ayuko. What if it was Ayuko who had been murdered? I'd always had my doubts about the existence of this Ayuko. As I mentioned earlier, right from the start I thought that O-Shige had a motive to kill Daigo, but I couldn't bring myself to believe that he would have a motive to kill her. For one, he was a parasite who'd made a living off O-Shige. Killing her would have been like killing the golden goose. But then again, perhaps, on the surface, Daigo might seem to have a motive for killing his wife. By that, I mean his new mistress, Ayuko. Were it not for her, it would be difficult to see what possible reason Daigo could have to murder O-Shige. In other words, it was only because of Ayuko that it was possible for O-Shige to pass herself off as having been murdered by her husband. It seemed almost too good to be true. So, I found myself wondering: mightn't this have been one of O-Shige's tricks as well? With that in mind, I began looking into this Ayuko and found that facts were rather thin on the ground. She'd worked in the Sunshine Dance Hall from May to June of last year. But from the time she stopped working there until the New Year, when she ran into an old colleague, nobody could say where she'd been or what she'd been doing. Then, this year, no sooner had she been spotted by O-Kimi, than the murder took place. This, too, seemed a little too convenient. What was clear was that there was a woman going by the name Ayuko. And it was also a fact that she knew Daigo, went to the cinema with him, and visited a strange house with him in Inokashira. But then I thought to myself: would a man like Daigo have another woman on the side? Not only did he make a living off his wife, but he was also clearly in love with her. The three women working at the Black Cat all testified to this. It was possible, of course, that he might have had a mistress, seeing as relations between men and women aren't always so straightforward. But here's what's strange. In the image of this couple that I have in my head, I very much doubt that O-Shige would be jealous even if Daigo did have an affair. I'd imagine she'd just look on coldly and sneer. And yet, O-Shige seemingly did get jealous. And what's more, she made a point of it in front of the girls. I thought to myself: there's something fishy there. So, I questioned the three girls about the pattern of events surrounding that, and the following came to light. Firstly, O-Shige's jealousy was a recent development, having begun only this year. Secondly, never once did she mention the name Ayuko. Instead, she always referred to her as "that girl" or "that woman". And thirdly, the way Daigo behaved in those situations was risible. He looked so foolish that it was hard to take it seriously. When I heard all this, I knew that there had to be some trickery on O-Shige's part, but at the time I never dreamt that she was performing such a masterpiece. It was the two diaries that made me realize that.'

Pausing to quench his thirst, Kosuke Kindaichi took another sip of beer before continuing with his story.

'The two diaries where those belonging to Kazama and O-Kimi. I suppose it isn't so strange that Kazama should keep a diary, but the fact that O-Kimi kept one without missing a single day for the past year is really quite something. Her diary, moreover, was the only clue to solving the strangest mystery of all, so all credit for this case should by rights go to O-Kimi. As you know, the Black Cat would close two or three times a month. But, according to O-Kimi's diary, until the end of last year O-Shige wouldn't

125

go to see Kazama on every one of those days off, but only once a month. On the other days off, she would either stay at home or go out with Daigo. It was only this year that she started going out every day off, claiming that she was going to see her lover. Kazama's diary, however, tells a rather different story. According to his one, he hadn't seen that much of O-Shige. They continued to see each other only once a month, just like last year. So, if O-Shige wasn't meeting Kazama, then where on earth was she going? What was even stranger was that recently, whenever O-Shige would go out, it was said that her husband would be sure to go out right after, but that, it transpired, wasn't always the case. There were instances when O-Shige would go out, but Daigo would sit at home quietly. And what's more, those were the days when O-Shige really did go and see Kazama. Then, on the days when we don't know where O-Shige went, her husband would always go out after she did. I met the dancer from the Sunshine Dance Hall and asked her if she could recall the day when she bumped into Ayuko in front of the National Theatre, and, lo and behold, that, too, was a day when O-Shige went out. It was the same story on the day when O-Kimi supposedly followed Ayuko. When I realized this, I was in a state of total shock. O-Shige and Ayuko were one and the same person. In other words, O-Shige was playing a double role. This isn't to say that I leapt to that conclusion in a single bound, but the more I thought about it, the more that conclusion became inescapable. I tested that hypothesis from all possible angles, trying to find anything that might contradict it, but it was watertight. The only person to have seen both O-Shige and Ayuko was O-Kimi, and, even then, she had only glimpsed Ayuko from afar in a crowd. But this was nothing more than an illusion. O-Shige usually did her hair in a traditional style and wore a sombre-coloured kimono, whereas Ayuko bobbed her hair and wore heavy make-up. It's little wonder that she was fooled. As for the others, those who knew O-Shige didn't know Ayuko, just as those who knew Ayuko didn't know O-Shige. What's more, the story that Ayuko had travelled back from China together with Daigo, and that she was his mistress, all came from O-Shige's lips. There was no other proof of it. And so, everything falls into place. In other words, to confect a situation in which her husband might kill her, O-Shige had to invent a motive for her husband. I was horrified when I realized this. I began to tremble. I wanted to close my eyes to it. I was afraid even to believe my own hypothesis. But that hypothesis was soon proved right. When I showed the people at the Sunshine Dance Hall a photograph of Hanako Matsuda, they said that although the girl in the picture had changed an awful lot, it had to be the same person. And, by the same stroke, having established that the girl in the photograph was a young O-Shige, we are left with the irrefutable fact that O-Shige was playing the part of two different people.'

Kosuke Kindaichi took another breather and stared intently into his beer glass. Nobody said a word. An awkward, heavy silence lingered in the room for a while, until at last the station chief and the chief inspector opened their mouths almost simultaneously.

'But how did O-Shige convince her husband to meet her for these strange lovers' trysts?' the station chief asked.

'And does this mean that O-Shige had been planning the murder since last May?' the chief inspector added.

'Yes,' said Kosuke Kindaichi. 'I think that's very likely. But let's start with the station chief's question. I doubt it would have been hard for O-Shige to pull it off. She might have said something like, "Oh, darling, I've been feeling a little low recently. Why don't we go out and pretend we're meeting again like we did last May? I'll reprise my role as Ayuko Kuwano and pretend that I've got myself a wealthy lover. I'll make eyes at you, and we'll have ourselves a little secret assignation. We've been in such a rut lately. We need a change of scenery. I need to be thrilled. Come on, say you will!" She'll have used all her charms to get her way with Daigo. And who knows? Maybe he himself enjoyed such games. Either way, he played right into O-Shige's hands.'

'Yes, I see,' said the station chief, nodding in admiration.

'As for the question about how long she'd been planning it, I can't prove it, but I suspect that Daigo must have tracked down O-Shige long before he paid Kazama a visit. Back then, O-Shige hadn't fleshed out her plan, but, as I suggested earlier, she'll have felt the desire to kill Daigo from the moment she laid eyes on him again, so her every step will have been taken with that goal in mind. When Daigo showed up, she'd have probably concealed her anger. "I have a lover these days," she might have said. "He's a real bigshot. He's got a lot of muscle, too. If he catches you meeting me here, there's no telling what he might do. So, you mustn't come here. I'll come and meet you…" And so, she came up with the fiction that was Ayuko Kuwano and would go out in disguise, claiming that she was trying not to be spotted by her lover or his henchmen. But then she'd have said, "You know, this can't go on forever, darling. One day my lover will find out, and he'll send me packing. So, to prepare for that day, I'm going to start dancing…" And anyway, Kazama had already fallen out of love with her by then. And what with his dozen or so other mistresses—'

'Don't talk rubbish!' said Kazama, wincing as he cut Kosuke Kindaichi off.

'What, it's two dozen these days, is it?' said the private detective, laughing. 'No, sorry, sorry! At any rate, Kazama was, at the time, visiting O-Shige less often, and so she was perfectly able to lead this kind of double-life. Before long, however, she found out about the existence of a woman called Chiyoko Ono. She got wind that her husband had returned to Japan with this woman and was still looking after her. But it was not out of the kindness of his heart, of course, that Daigo did so. No, it was his intention to sell her into prostitution sooner or later, but O-Shige thought up another way of putting her to use.

'Back then, O-Shige's plan was a simple one. Namely, to kill Daigo and pin the blame on this poor Ono girl. At first, she wanted to give the other dancers the impression that she was Ono. Incidentally, I asked the dancer that saw the suitcase with the initials C.O. on it, and she said that it was big and so loud that you could tell at first glance that it was a woman's. But Chiyoko Ono had travelled south from Manchuria, smearing her face with dirt and pretending to be a man, so there's no way that she could have taken that case with her – it would have made her disguise useless. So, even before I realized that O-Shige and Ayuko were the same person, I knew that Ayuko the dancer was not Chiyoko Ono. So, O-Shige had made a plan but at the time lacked the courage to carry it out. Killing a person, and a man at that, is no small undertaking for a woman. But while she was waiting patiently for the right moment, she was also plotting. And just then, someone suitable appeared on the scene. And that someone was Nitcho.'

Kosuke Kindaichi paused and shuddered violently, as though an insect had fallen down his back. Looking just as grim-faced, the others sighed heavily.

'As you are aware, gentlemen,' Kosuke Kindaichi continued, 'the glass panels of the shoji doors at the back of the Black Cat are pasted over with paper. Only, they were not papered recently, but shortly after Daigo and O-Shige moved in last year. The reason for this, as O-Kimi explained, was that the monk couldn't help peeping down at O-Shige from the bank overlooking the back garden. "He's a bit of a card, that one," she said. "Maybe he's even some kind of pervert." Whatever the case, O-Shige turned this to her advantage. In other words, she used her wiles and made Nitcho her accomplice. As I mentioned previously, the only thing that contradicted my hypothesis was the monk's testimony. However, as I became more and more convinced that my hypothesis had to be right, I could only think that Nitcho was lying. At first, I wondered whether he hadn't perhaps been taken in, seeing O-Shige disguised as Ayuko, but gradually I realized that everything he did was awfully convenient for O-Shige's plan. His testimony was made to look as though he'd been forced to tell the truth when Tamekichi pointed out the inconsistencies in his original story, but even without Tamekichi, he'd been planning to make another statement at some point. As for the timing of his digging up the body, then why, if his story were true, wouldn't he have exhumed the corpse on the 14th or 15th, when the Black Cat was empty? If the body had been dug up then, the degree of decomposition wouldn't have been so severe, and we would have been able to identify the deceased. In other words, the monk was waiting until this would no longer be possible. I also think I can say with confidence that the body was not buried there. Until the night of the 14th, only the black cat was buried in the garden. So, where was the body? It was in the graveyard, where we later found Daigo's corpse. The body was initially buried there, and then, in the small hours of the 20th, when it was so decomposed that it might well be mistaken for O-Shige's, Nitcho exhumed the body and moved it to the back garden of the Black Cat, where he set about burying it once again. In other words, what Constable Hasegawa discovered was not the monk digging up the body but burying it! He knew, of course, that Hasegawa made his rounds every night at around that time, and the sooner the police began their investigation, the sooner they would come to suspect Daigo.'

The men all sighed heavily again. It was a dark feeling, devoid of any comfort.

'Now, I've gone back and forth on this a little, but ever since O-Shige found a suitable accomplice, she had begun to draw up a new plan. As half a year had passed, though, it was a lot more complicated than her previous one. The first thing she did was to make herself appear to be the murder victim. Next, she had to kill her husband in secret and hide the body somewhere so that she could pin the suspicion on him. As the instrument by which she would carry out this plan—or rather, the victim—she had previously chosen Chiyoko Ono. By this point, Daigo had sold Chiyoko into prostitution, but O-Shige knew where to find her. When she was sold, Chiyoko had been so ashamed that she hid her real name, so even if her name appeared in the papers later, the house where she was kept—a brothel—would never have noticed, and so O-Shige could rest easy. As I intimated earlier, not only did she create the illusion of this woman called Ayuko by playing two roles, but she also feigned jealousy in order to make it seem more believable. And yet, never once did she mention her name. As I said before, she'd just say "that girl" or "that woman". So, her husband thought she was talking about Chiyoko Ono, while O-Kimi and the other two women thought she was talking about Ayuko. Oh yes, she was very clever to pull that off as well as she did.'

Kosuke Kindaichi paused for a moment to collect his thoughts.

'I'm afraid this has been a rather long and winding story, gentlemen, so I'll do my best to make it as simple as possible from now on. You don't need me to tell you, but, the preparatory working having been completed, it's finally time to get down to the heart of the matter. On that fateful night, the 28th of February, while Daigo was away, purchasing supplies, O-Shige summoned poor Chiyoko Ono to the Black Cat Cafe and killed her with a single blow. I don't know whether it was O-Shige or Nitcho who actually dealt it, but it amounts to much the same, either way. Nitcho then carried the body to the graveyard, where he buried it, while O-Shige killed the black cat in order to trick her husband. She was also careful to leave the parasol that O-Kimi had seen "Ayuko" carrying under the table in the bar. Then she smeared her face with greasepaint to bring on the allergic reaction and withdrew to her room. This was murder number one, but the frightening thing is that this murder was not really O-Shige's aim. Rather, it was merely a prelude to murder number two, which happened next. And that took place two weeks later, on the evening of the 14th.

'After leaving the Black Cat, Daigo and O-Shige passed by the police box in G—— Town and immediately ducked into the Renge-in. I don't know on what pretext she dragged her husband in there, but she could have come up with any number of excuses. It was there that Daigo was killed, and, this time, I think it's beyond doubt that it was Nitcho who did the deed. After burying the body in the graveyard, O-Shige decided to hide for the time being in the temple storehouse. They do say that it's hard to see what's under your own nose, and this was truly an excellent hiding place. Thus began O-Shige's strange life in the storehouse, but she had made one miscalculation. And this was that Nitcho wasn't as simple as he appeared to be. Previously, O-Shige had taken advantage of Nitcho's eccentricities and his obsession with her to manipulate him, but now those same eccentricities became a danger for her. Now, at last, the monk was able to have O-Shige all to himself. He never let his guard down and refused to let O-Shige leave the storehouse, even after she wanted to flee. And that is what led to O-Shige's downfall.'

There ended Kosuke Kindaichi's story. For several moments, the men just stared blankly in front of them, not daring to say a word. It looked as if none of them could bring himself to speak.

'What on earth was she planning to do about Nitcho, I wonder?' murmured Murai after a while.

'I doubt he would have been long for this world,' Kosuke Kindaichi responded in as off-hand a manner as he could muster. But even so, he could not suppress the trembling in his voice. 'Once the heat had died down, a body with a shaven head would have been discovered somewhere. Only then would O-Shige have been able to rest easy and start her new life.' He then turned to the station chief. 'Incidentally, what has become of Nitcho?'

The chief shook his head gloomily.

'It's not good. When he arrived at the station yesterday, he realized that he'd been tricked. Apparently, he became violent, and when everyone tried to stop him, he suddenly started foaming at the mouth and collapsed… His strange love life with O-Shige must have had a powerful effect on him. He regained consciousness, but it's been impossible to get any sense out of him ever since.'

The men sighed heavily once again and remained silent for some time. In the end, it was Kazama who, as if to break the leaden atmosphere, spoke up in a cheerful voice.

'Well, gentlemen, I don't know about you, but this gruesome case has taken it out of me. Allow me to offer you something hot to exorcize the evil spirits.'

And, with that, he clapped his hands.

EPILOGUE

And so, as this sinister record reaches its end, permit me to conclude by quoting from another a letter that I received from Kosuke Kindaichi.

My dear Y——, I suppose, in the end, this case did not stray too far from your 'faceless corpse' formula, but it was certainly complicated by the fact that there was another trick at play—that of one person playing two roles. You once told me that the 'double role' was a trick that should be kept secret right until the very end, and that if the reader worked it out, the author had failed. This was true not only of the novel, but also, in this case, of the incident itself. The moment I realized that Ayuko and O-Shige were, in fact, one and the same person, O-Shige had lost. But tell me, my dear Y——, were you able to work it all out for yourself?

Frankly speaking, no, I wasn't. But how about you, dear reader?

WHY DID THE WELL WHEEL CREAK?

MEMORANDUM CONCERNING
THE HONIDEN FAMILY

On the close resemblance between
Daisuke Honiden and Goichi Akizuki

The Honiden family cemetery is situated on the hillside that embraces the village of K——.

This modestly sized plot, which is surrounded by a black wooden fence, is always kept immaculately clean, and the gravestones of generation upon generation of the Honiden family stand there, lined up in neat rows. Strange though it may seem, whenever I see this group of imposing gravestones, I cannot help picturing the various members of that august family, decked out in all their finery, sitting solemnly upright in the formal fashion.

The tenants of these graves must surely be lamenting the recent deeds of their descendants. And is it just my imagination, or does that gravestone at the very end of the line not even look a trifle ashamed? Come to think of it, was it not the tenant of that particular grave, Daizaburo Honiden—who passed on to the next life on the 20th of

March 1933—who sowed the seeds of these recent events more than twenty years ago?

Now, as I publish this series of letters relating the particulars of those harrowing events—letters that came into my possession quite by chance—I should like to take the opportunity to say a few words about this Daizaburo and also about the social standing of the Honiden family.

Originally, the Honiden family, together with the Ono and the Akizuki families, comprised the 'three great houses' of the village of K——, and, in the old days of the shogun, the Honiden family held the important hereditary role of village chieftains. Later, after the Meiji Restoration, even though the family lost that status, it continued to prosper—or rather, it would be more accurate to say that it flourished—while the Ono and the Akizuki families fell into decline. The reasons for this were several, but the principle among them was probably that, whereas the other two families failed to produce any men of quality, the Honidens produced one fine figure after another.

One in particular, a certain Yasuke, the head of the family during the Restoration itself, was a shrewd businessman and, according to legend, took advantage of all the chaos at the time to transfer a sizeable portion of the former daimyo's estate into his own name, under the guise of liquidating government assets.

His heir, a man by the name of Shojiro, was a sober and reliable sort of fellow. He, too, was adept at making money and would lend it at eye-wateringly high rates of interest; if the repayments were even so much as a day late, he would repossess people's houses, their farmland and even their woodland.

One version of the story holds that the decline of the Ono and Akizuki families was not only due to their having produced one feckless head of the family after another, but also spurred on by the punitive rates of interest charged by Shojiro on his loans, which by the early 1910s had resulted in most of the farmland belonging to both houses, along with countless heirlooms and family treasures being appropriated by the Honiden family.

When Shojiro died in 1914, Daizaburo took over as head of the family at the age of twenty-eight. He was married but had no children, and, given that two generations had passed since Yasuke improved the family's fortune, he was every bit the magnanimous and generous sort of man that a third-generation head of a prosperous family tends to be. He enjoyed lively gatherings, indulged in all kinds of recreation, kept the company of actors and artists, and was a patron to many; yet seemingly the blood of his forebears still flowed through his veins, and so he did nothing that might deplete the riches that his house had acquired. In short, despite his love of ostentation, Daizaburo, too, was an astute man.

In those days, the Ono family had fallen irrevocably on hard times and moved, lock, stock and barrel to Kobe.

The Akizukis, however, were just about managing to keep afloat, and the then-head of the family was a man called Zentaro. He was Daizaburo's senior by seven years, and, like most descendants of a ruined noble family, he was utterly incompetent when it came to managing his affairs. Dubbing himself 'a man of letters', he spent his days immersed in poetry, making dreadful 'literati' paintings and practising his calligraphy by writing poems on slips of paper, which he would then take to show Daizaburo. Whenever the latter would condescend to buy this piece of calligraphy, Zentaro would make a solemn and clumsy show of flattery, only then to return home in a foul temper, cursing his benefactor and lashing out at his own wife, O-Ryu, who thought that the whole business was shameful.

O-Ryu was a quiet, gentle soul, rather pretty, and she would teach the other girls in the village how to sew, how to perform the tea ceremony, and how to arrange flowers. People said that she was too good for her husband, and this only infuriated Zentaro further.

'My wife isn't happy with me,' he would think. 'She despises me.'

As these thoughts assailed him, Zentaro's blood would seethe, he would beat his wife at the drop of a hat, and, on occasion, he would even drag her out into the street by the hair. Whenever this happened, O-Ryu would not even dare to raise her voice, for fear that the neighbours might hear. Her forbearance only enraged Zentaro further.

The couple had a girl named O-Rin. With her frizzy hair and dearth of charm, she was a gloomy sort of child. In 1917, when O-Rin was six years old, Zentaro had a stroke, which left one side of his body paralysed. Until then, the family had managed to scrape by on a small income, but afterwards their years of penury overtook them, and they found themselves in dire straits. With an invalid to look after, O-Ryu seemed to wither away in both body and soul.

Unable to stand idly by, Daizaburo would come to see Zentaro often, each time leaving some money behind. As ever, whenever he would receive his guest, Zentaro would shower him with the most cringing flattery, but then, the very moment the man left, he would shower him with curses. And yet, never once did he return the money that Daizaburo had left him.

The year after Zentaro's stroke—that is, in 1918—both Daizaburo's wife and O-Ryu fell pregnant around the same time. Then, the following spring, the two women were both delivered of baby boys a month apart. However, on the seventh night after the Akizuki boy—the first of the two—arrived, Zentaro hauled his partially paralysed body out of bed and flung himself down a well.

If only you had seen the child to which O-Ryu gave birth, you would understand immediately why Zentaro did what he did. The baby had polycoria in both eyes. And who else should have had this rare condition but Daizaburo Honiden? Indeed, when Daizaburo himself was born, his grandfather Yasuke, who was still alive at the time, was overjoyed at this, reputedly saying, 'The child has double pupils! He will surely make the Honiden name famous the whole world over. We must raise him with all due care.'

Ever since he had taken over as head of the family at a young age, Daizaburo had been wont to indulge his every whim, although he managed this without being taken advantage of by others. This was partly due to the charm he possessed, but it was also on account of the legend surrounding him, which singled him out as special and lent him an air of menace. This, coupled with the fact that Zentaro and his wife had probably not enjoyed relations since his stroke, made it clear that the child born to O-Ryu was, in all likelihood, Daizaburo's—and so it is little wonder that Zentaro killed himself in a pique of rage after being confronted with this explicit evidence of his wife's adultery.

People in the countryside tend to take a rather relaxed attitude to these things. When it comes to men, in particular, dalliances such as these are often ignored, although women do find themselves the subject of a certain degree of criticism. The fact that her husband had died on account of her infidelity meant that O-Ryu found herself at the sharp end of public scorn. For a whole year, she had to endure their cuts and barbs. Then, after waiting for Goichi (for that was the name that she gave to the child) to wean, she left him and his sister O-Rin, who was coming up to her eighth birthday, with a distant, elderly relative. Then, on the anniversary of her husband's death, she threw herself into the same well. She left no suicide note behind, but it was said that she must have done this to atone for her sin.

Daizaburo's wife named her boy Daisuke. By the time that Daisuke and Goichi had reached the age of five or six, it was clear to everyone that they were brothers. Even though they had been born to different mothers, they looked like two peas in a pod. The only difference was that, while Goichi had polycoria, Daisuke did not. And so, by the time that they were in their fifth or sixth year of primary school—the point at which they resembled each other most closely—the only way to tell them apart was by looking at their eyes.

Later on, their similarity began to fade, however, and by the time the boys reached twenty, they no longer resembled one another. This very likely had something to do with their circumstances and their environment. After leaving school, Daisuke went on to study at a technical college in Osaka, and, having been given free rein in life as the eldest scion of the Honiden family, he grew into a well-built, attractive young man who was full of charm.

Goichi, on the other hand, who from his tender years had to work in the fields alongside his sister, O-Rin, was skeletally thin and had a dark complexion to match his brusque demeanour.

What with their scant sense of propriety, countryfolk have a habit of relishing the scandals of others, and so

Goichi knew the scandal surrounding his birth from an early age. And this only made his character grimmer still.

'We share the same father,' Goichi would think, feeling a visceral sense of resentment, 'so why is it that Daisuke can lead a happy, carefree life, while I've been saddled with this wretched one of poverty? After all, I'm a whole month older than Daisuke, so by rights, as the eldest son, I should be able to stake my claim to the Honiden family fortune. Why must I be forsaken like this?! Why must I work, covered in sweat and blisters, while Daisuke is out enjoying life?'

It was O-Rin who fanned the flames of Goichi's unassuageable, bitter resentment. Ever since she had been old enough to understand, O-Rin had been schooled in her father Zentaro's loathing of the Honiden family. And so now, like a tattoo artist pricking him with a needle, she tried to instil in Goichi that hatred she had learnt from her father. Revenge upon the Honiden family, a curse upon Daizaburo—for as long as he could remember, those crazy oaths were all Goichi had ever heard from his sister.

What O-Rin appeared to have neglected, however, was that Goichi was none other than the son of Daizaburo, and a blood member of the Honiden family. And so, all these curses and calls for revenge seemed to have little effect on Goichi. If anything, he had a strong yearning to be closer to the Honiden family. In only one respect did he share his sister's thoughts, and that was their mutual hatred for Daisuke. Whenever he thought about Daisuke, he felt as if his whole body were about to burst into flames. Goichi simply loathed him through and through.

Meanwhile, two more children appeared in the Honiden family. A second son, Shinkichi, was born in 1922, and a daughter, Tsuruyo, followed in 1930. There had in fact been two other children born between them, but as they both died in their infancy, we shall not count them here.

The girl, Tsuruyo, was a very unfortunate creature. Born with a congenital heart defect, she would be left breathless by even the slightest exertion, and so she was practically confined to her room. Naturally, it would have been unthinkable to send her to school when she reached the appropriate age, and so it was decided to tutor her at home, instead. Her education was provided mostly by her grandmother, O-Maki, on whose knee the girl learnt the rudiments of reading and writing. She turned out to be a bright child and, by the age of twelve or thereabouts, she had begun reading annotated editions of classics such as *The Cavern of the Disporting Fairies* and *The Tale of Genji*.

As is recorded on his gravestone, Daizaburo died in 1933—that is, when Tsuruyo was three years old. His wife who survived him was a quiet, unassuming woman and quite unsuited to the business of running a family, and so it was reliable old O-Maki who in the end had to shoulder the burden of responsibility. Her stalwart character, instilled in her by her own late husband, Shojiro, helped to sustain the fortunes of that august clan.

Daisuke married immediately after leaving school, in 1941. The brutal impact of the war was being felt ever more acutely, and many families now arranged their sons' marriages as hastily as possible. His bride, Rie, hailed from the neighbouring village and was the daughter of a respectable old samurai family fallen on hard times. Rumour had it that she had in fact been in love with Goichi but, upon receiving an unexpected proposal of marriage from the young scion of the Honiden family, had no qualms about trading up. If this was true, it can have only stoked Goichi's hatred for Daisuke.

The year after Daisuke's marriage, both he and Goichi were simultaneously called up for military service. They joined the same unit and were stationed first somewhere along the Yangtze. There, in that far-flung foreign land, Goichi appeared to forget his old grudge and, by all accounts, the two of them seemed to get along well. According to a letter that Daisuke sent his wife, Rie, at the time, they were prized by the unit as their twin mascots, and, as proof, he enclosed a photograph of the two of them side by side—although this image would cast a very eerie shadow over the events that took place later.

I happened to see that photo myself once, and, as I turned over those terrible events in my mind, I could not help but shudder.

A physical resemblance had returned to the two men. Perhaps it was the circumstances that had evened out their bodies. Before being called up, Daisuke had been well-built and fair-skinned, but now the hardships of war had taken their toll: he had lost weight, and his face had been burnt by the sun. Goichi, on the other hand, had managed to put on a little weight, and his dark tan had faded somewhat. And so, once again the two of them met in the middle, so alike that they might have been taken for the same person. The only point of difference was the uncanny glitter that came from the double pupils of Goichi's eyes...

Later, in 1943, Shinkichi, the younger son of the Honiden family, left school to fight. He found himself discharged within six months, however, after contracting tuberculosis. He convalesced at home for a little over a year, and then, shortly after the war ended, he entered the H—— Tuberculosis Sanatorium, which was located some fifteen miles from the village of K——.

Perhaps from despondency over the fact that both of her sons had been drafted into the army, Shinkichi's mother died in the autumn of 1943, and so, when he entered the sanatorium, he left five people behind in the vast Honiden mansion: his grandmother, O-Maki; his sister-in-law, Rie; his younger sister, Tsuruyo; the family's longstanding housekeeper, O-Sugi; and a somewhat backwards manservant, Shikazo. It was for this reason that Shinkichi would come back to visit only once or twice a month, staying for a couple of nights at a time. And while the sanatorium was only fifteen miles from the village of K——, because of poor transportation links, you had to transfer from a branch line with infrequent services to a narrow-gauge railway, before then taking a bus, and so even if you were to leave early in the morning, very often you would not arrive there until the evening. It was impossible to make the round trip in a day.

Shinkichi adored his younger sister. He was of a literary bent himself and fully intended to become a writer someday, but he valued Tsuruyo's talent more highly than his own and seems to have wanted to mould his sister into a writer like Emily Brontë. Because of her heart condition, the girl spent her time hidden away in the storehouse, immersed in books, but she had a strong sensitivity and a keen eye for observation.

Shinkichi instructed his sister to write to him at the sanatorium from time to time, no matter whether she had any news or not. His aim in this, it seems, was to train her eye as well as to hone her penmanship. And so, Tsuruyo wrote letters to her brother dutifully, just as he had asked.

From the end of 1944 to the beginning of 1945, there were many changes in K——, as was the case in every other village across Japan. As air raids on the cities became more frequent, those who had previously left the village now returned in dribs and drabs as evacuees—and this included the Ono family.

The head of the Ono family was a man named Uichiro. He had run a stationery shop in Kobe, but now, having been bombed out, he was forced to return to the village for the first time in thirty years. Uichiro had been in his twenties when he left, and so now he was an old man with a full head of white hair. He brought with him his second wife, O-Saki, and their five children, the eldest of whom was sixteen. Uichiro also had a son, Shoji, from his first marriage, but the boy had been drafted into the army and his whereabouts were unknown.

Fortunately, the Ono house had been left in the care of a relative, so it had been repaired to the extent that it did not leak; they were also able to take back a little plot of land that had been given over to a tenant farmer and begin farming it themselves.

In August 1945, shortly after the war ended, Goichi's elder sister, O-Rin, returned to the village. She was thirty-five but still unmarried. Throughout the war, she had worked as a cook in a munitions factory in a neighbouring town, but when the war ended, she lost her job and had to come back, only to find herself living in what was little more than a cowshed and working a tiny patch of land. She had always been a quiet woman, but this recent spate of bad luck had made her turn in on herself so much that people might well have thought her a recluse or even a witch.

With the main characters of this story now more or less assembled, Daisuke returned unexpectedly in the summer of 1946. Naturally, his being demobbed was a source of untold joy for the Honiden family, but, in spite of this, he also brought back with him an indescribable sense of horror and dread.

As I look around the Honiden cemetery once again, I see, at the end of this orderly row of gravestones commemorating generation upon generation of the family, a little mound at the foot of a crape myrtle in a blaze of scarlet, and above that mound a still-new wooden post bearing the posthumous name of one of the family's children. If you look at the back, you will see that it reads: TSURUYO HONIDEN, WHO DIED 15 OCTOBER 1946. This is the temporary grave of that lovely girl, and it goes without saying that it was the shock of those horrific events that robbed her of her life.

Before she died, however, she wrote regularly to her brother Shinkichi, sparing no detail, and relaying all her thoughts, impressions and speculations about what happened. Of course, her letters were not written to report these goings-on from the very outset. As I have already mentioned, she was in the habit of writing to her brother about all manner of things that occurred in her life. Yet once that fateful night came to pass, it very naturally became the focus of her letters, and she went on to relate at length the terrible suspicions, the sequence of events and, ultimately, the alarming discovery that stole away her life.

Every time I read over her letters, I cannot but shudder at the harrowing things to befall this young lady of only seventeen years of age—such do they bear the imprint of her sorrow and anguish.

The story you are about to read is comprised of a bundle of Tsuruyo's letters to her brother, although it was in fact from Kosuke Kindaichi that I acquired them. In addition to them, the private detective also furnished me with several newspaper clippings and a postscript written by another figure in this tale.

'I'd like to make it clear from the outset that I had nothing to do with this case whatsoever,' he told me as he handed the materials over. There was a darkness in his eyes. 'Or rather, I was on the point of involving myself in it. But then, just as I'd worked out the truth and was about to make an approach to the culprit, it turned out that somebody with a more perceptive mind than my own had already made the identification, and so I took my leave without saying a word. If you read to the end, however, you will come to understand how these documents came into my possession. You will find that I have numbered them, but I have not organized them in any particular way. That I leave entirely to you.'

Following Kosuke Kindaichi's advice, I have extracted only the parts of Tsuruyo's letters that are directly relevant to the case, and I have lightly edited them, adding a few words here and there to make them easier to read.

And so, with that little disclaimer out of the way, let us now turn to these letters that Tsuruyo wrote. The first one was written in May 1946, about five months before the incident took place.

THE SORROWS OF KUZUNOHA

On a folding screen depicting the
kitsune *Kuzunoha without any eyes*

3 MAY 1946

There was such an awful to-do here yesterday. I imagine you
will have heard already that Mr Ono and his family have
been evacuated back to the village. Well, yesterday the old
man came to pick a quarrel.

Did you know that we have a folding screen at home with
a painting of the *kitsune* fox-spirit Kuzunoha? I myself had
no idea until just yesterday. It has been locked away in the
storehouse, but for as long as I can recall I have never seen
it displayed. I did not even know that we had such a screen.

Well, anyway, this screen was the reason for the old man's
visit. In short, he wanted it back.

'I left that screen with Daisuke thirty years ago when I
set off for Kobe,' he said. 'I gave it to him for safekeeping,
and not as a gift or anything of the sort! That screen is a
family heirloom that's been passed down from one generation of the Onos to the next. No matter what else I may

have lost, I cannot part with that! And besides, now that I've returned to the land of my ancestors, I'd very much like to reclaim that screen and spend the remainder of my days contemplating it.'

How he kept harping on this, repeating the same thing over and over, until people could stand it no longer. He tried his luck first with Rie, but, realizing that he was getting nowhere with her, he eventually moved on to Grandmother. She became really quite indignant.

'What on earth are you talking about, Uichiro?' she said. 'Why, I remember that screen only too well. Back when you were about to leave for Kobe, business hadn't been going so well and you were short on cash, so you asked for twenty yen and left us this in exchange. What was it you said, back then? No matter how important your ancestors were to you, you couldn't carry a big screen like that all the way to Kobe? "Please, have this for your home," I remember you saying quite clearly. Don't you think it's a bit much to ask for it back now?'

Grandmother certainly gave him what for, but the old man was undeterred, and, after repeating the same thing and being rebuffed yet again, he resigned himself and simply said, 'Well, in that case, I'll return the money I borrowed from you.' And with that he laid down two ten-yen notes!

I was flabbergasted. Has the old man not heard of inflation? Prices nowadays are tens if not hundreds of times what they were before the war. Can he seriously believe that

156

twenty yen from thirty years ago is the same as twenty yen today? It seemed so absurd that even I was affronted by it.

Grandmother had the following to say about it all afterwards.

'Poverty may make people do strange things, but even though Uichiro appears to have changed somewhat, he isn't the sort of man to try his hand at extortion. It's all that O-Saki's fault. She must have heard about that folding screen somewhere and put him up to it. Otherwise, why would he come looking for it more than a year after returning to the village? It's nice to see a familiar face in the village again, but with outsiders like O-Saki it's difficult to know where you stand. Ever since the war, people have become more and more unscrupulous, so you, Rie, you've got to be as hard as nails—otherwise you'll come a cropper.'

I do not mean simply to parrot Grandmother's views, but that O-Saki really does have a reputation that precedes her. Apparently, she worked in Kobe as a barmaid or something of the kind. And they say that it was none other than she who bullied her stepson, Shoji, so much that he had to leave home. It made a complete delinquent of him, and, even after he was drafted into the army, there is no telling how many days and nights he had to spend in the detention barracks. Or so people say, at least. Speaking of Shoji, he came back soon after the war ended, but before three days were out, he had a blazing row with O-Saki and ran off again. And yet, I have also heard it said that Shoji once gave old man Ono some money to stop him selling the family house. That is seemingly why everybody in the village pities poor Shoji. There was a rumour going around that he was a burglar in K—— City, but even if that is true, I still feel awfully sorry for him.

4 MAY 1946

I was too tired to finish my letter yesterday, especially after digressing so much, so today I shall pick up where I left off and tell you all about the folding screen with the painting of Kuzunoha.

As I was saying, old man Ono just kept repeating himself over and over, so much so that even I began to get annoyed with him, but, when all was said and done, Grandmother just gave him short shrift, and in the end he had no choice but to give up and go home. He had made me so, so angry, saying all those tedious things, but when I saw him shuffle dejectedly off, I somehow felt sorry for him. He cut such a pathetic figure. His waistband was all tattered and frayed and done in such an unkempt fashion. He has changed so very much since his last trip back to visit the family cemetery; it almost brought a tear to my eyes.

I have to wonder, though: what if only Rie and I had been at home? There would surely have been tears if he had kept on at us like that. Truly, I do not know where this house would be, if it were not for Grandmother. She is as strong as an ox and as stubborn as ever; but even so, she is seventy-eight now. I cannot help worrying what the future holds. After all, we are still waiting for news about Daisuke's whereabouts, and so you, Brother, are the only person I can turn to. Please, get well soon.

There I go, letting my brush run away from me again. Forgive me. It is hard to imagine such an undisciplined writer ever becoming a novelist!

After Ono left, Grandmother seemed to be perturbed by something and just sat there in silence with her eyes closed for a while. Eventually, she opened them and turned to Rie.

'Go and find O-Sugi,' she said, 'and have her fetch that folding screen from the storehouse.'

Rie looked a little taken aback.

'You mean...?'

'Yes, yes, the one with the image of Kuzunoha. O-Sugi will for sure know the one I mean. Give her a hand to bring it here, won't you?'

I was curious, so I asked, 'Grandmother, are going to give the screen back to Mr Ono?'

But all she said was 'No'—and not another word.

Rie and O-Sugi returned before long, carrying the screen in question. Truth be told, I had been awfully curious to see it from the moment the old man mentioned it. After all, I had never even heard of its existence it before, but he made it sound like something really special. So, you can imagine how I held my breath as it was borne in and the oil cloth covering it was carefully removed.

Have you ever seen that folding screen, Brother? I doubt it. Grandmother said that it had not been displayed in a long time, so I am certain that you will not even have heard of it before. The very moment I set eyes on it, a strange feeling came over me. It is difficult to say why exactly, but all of a sudden my whole body went numb and my heart started pounding.

The screen is in two panels, with the depiction of Kuzunoha on the left-hand side. It looks like the scene in which she bids farewell to her son, forsakes her husband and returns to the Forest of Shinoda. She is depicted with both sleeves drawn together in front of her, her head bowed slightly, and the back of her neck elongated. The painting has been executed very carefully, using a mixture of delicate lines and artist's chalk, and the hem of her kimono blurs into the autumn foliage below. Then, on the right-hand panel, there is just a faint sliver of a crescent moon, no more than a thread's breadth. The background is covered in mica glitter, and its dull lustre seems to capture the loneliness and melancholy of Abeno by night.

Unlike other paintings of Kuzunoha that I have seen, there is no fox depicted anywhere on this folding screen. Kuzunoha herself has no fox's tail, either. And yet, curiously enough, that slender figure depicted standing there does have some rather fox-like features. The lower half of her body, with the hem of her kimono trailing in the autumn leaves, left me with the distinct impression that she was already turning back into a fox. It was quite eerie, in fact. Trying to put my finger on the reason for this, I took a closer look at the figure, and that was when I noticed something startling.

Kuzunoha may be shown looking sorrowful and with her head downcast, but her eyes are wide open. And neither of them has been painted in. If the finishing touches are the most important part of a painting, then looking at this one will really show you just how important the eyes are to a human face.

As I stood there, staring at the painting, I was suddenly reminded of the puppets used in the *bunraku* theatre. The one used for the role of Miyuki in the play *The Tale of the Morning Glory* had its eyes completely inverted, so that only the whites were showing. This painting of Kuzunoha is just like that. Truly, it has an indescribably sinister air about it.

Was it by accident, I wonder, that the artist neglected to add in the eyes? Or did he know the effect it would produce and leave them out on purpose? For some reason, I cannot help thinking that it must have been the latter.

Rie also held her breath as she examined the painting, but then I noticed her shuddering.

'What a creepy painting,' she muttered.

Grandmother looked at her curiously and asked, 'Oh? What makes you say that?'

'Well, it's just that I've never seen Kuzunoha blind before... What do you make of it, Tsuruyo?'

Rie's question caught me off-guard. I am used to talking about that sort of thing with you, of course, Brother, but being asked this all of a sudden by Rie flustered me. I cannot say why. After all, I have always thought Rie to be a kind soul, and I like her more than words or my brush can express. And yet, whenever the two of us are alone together, I freeze, and whenever she speaks to me, I go to pieces. It must be because she is so pretty.

'Yes, you're right... I don't think I've seen her blind before, either,' was all the answer I could muster.

For a little while, Grandmother said nothing and just looked at the screen. Then she said, 'So, it's the eyes that are troubling you both, is it? But this merely reflects the artist's careful thinking about the subject matter. After all, what this painting shows isn't the real Princess Kuzunoha. It's the fox-spirit who's taken on her form. Moreover, her true identity has just been exposed, and so here she's shown slinking off to the Forest of Shinoda. The artist who painted this hasn't shown her with a fox's tail or anything, but in leaving out the eyes he's indicating that this Kuzunoha isn't human. Whenever I see this painting, I cannot help admiring it.'

Grandmother said all this, her eyes narrowed in contemplation of the screen in front of her, but now she turned to the two of us and added, 'I think we'll leave the screen here for the time being… Oh, it isn't that I'm so very fond of it. It's just that if we were to hide it away in the store-house again after all that rubbish Uichiro was saying, then people might think we were up to something underhand or trying to keep it a secret. So, let's keep it here in full view for people to see.'

And that is how the Kuzunoha folding screen came to adorn the formal sitting room. So, the next time you come home, Brother, you will be able to see it for yourself in all its uncanny glory…

DAISUKE RETURNS

On Shoji Ono's escape

10 JUNE 1946

The village is astir with several rumours of which I must inform you, Brother.

Just yesterday, three strange men turned up at old man Ono's place and went barging in with the most menacing looks on their faces. Apparently, they were officers from the prison in O—— City, and it is thanks to them that we have finally learnt what has become of Shoji.

It seems that he was being held in the city pending trial for robbery. Perhaps because he was afraid of word getting out, or perhaps because there are other crimes hanging over him, he gave them a false name: something Oshima. Only, as the trial date drew nearer, he realized that he would not be able to get away with using a false name, so he and half a dozen other prisoners plotted a prison-break by removing the floorboards. All the other men were found soon enough and placed back in custody, but this 'Oshima' managed to escape.

So, when the officers at the prison in O—— made inquiries into the background of this Mr 'Oshima', they discovered that there was no such man, and it was only then that they realized he had given them an alias. When they questioned the other prisoners, they learnt that Oshima had let slip that he had once served time in a penal colony on Y—— Island, so a call was immediately placed there. While the penal colony on the island apparently had no record of any man by the name of Oshima, they were nevertheless able to identify the fugitive as Shoji Ono by his physical characteristics. The conclusive evidence was that Shoji had a tattoo on one arm, which read: GUN FOR HIRE, LIFE FOR SALE.

Having learnt all this, the officers then headed directly to old man Ono's house. Apparently, they are responsible for escaped prisoners for the first forty-eight hours, or something like that, and so they kept watch there until ten o'clock this morning, after which they left.

Still, I cannot help feeling sorry for poor Shoji. From what I understand, they believe that he and two of his associates formed a gang that staged those robberies in Y—— three months ago. And apparently it happened there again: Shoji's two associates were apprehended, while he himself was the only one to escape. The police were already on the lookout for him, so, when he was arrested for something else, he must have decided to try to pass himself off under an assumed name. But no matter how far you run, you will never manage to outrun Fate. A man's crimes always catch up with him in the end. But the locals still sympathize with him, all the same. O-Saki drove him out of his own home and put him in the care of some relatives in the village for several years. He was never the same after that. He was a deeply sensitive boy and prone to tears, but everybody says that this was O-Saki's doing, and so they all hate her. It is quite true, I assure you. If I remember rightly, dear Brother, you and he are around the same age and were once good friends. So, you probably know more about Shoji than I do.

Speaking of O-Saki... She came here a couple of times, asking about that screen, but Grandmother sent her packing each time. She has not darkened our door again lately, so perhaps she has given up on the idea. Apparently, she has let it be known that, if she finds Shoji, she will place a rope around his neck and drag him to the local police station herself. What a truly hateful woman.

In other news, O-Rin is stealing wood from our land, as usual. That lot never changes. I know that, compared to our family, she and Goichi are in an unfortunate position, so I try to turn a blind eye to it, but recently she has become so very brazen, stealing not only the firewood we would ordinarily use ourselves, but also the wood that is earmarked for sale. Shikazo was so terribly angry about it all that yesterday he staked her out and caught her red-handed.

'The land itself has been stolen,' I am told she retorted quite shamelessly. 'Originally, it was ours until the Honidens swindled us out of it...'

The woman lives next to the cemetery, in a little cottage that is scarcely bigger than a cowshed. It must be awfully frightening to be alone in such a desolate place.

On another note, did you know that the Yoshidas' boy, Ginzo, has finally got married? Only, who do you suppose the bride is? It is his own sister-in-law, Kanae. Her husband, Yasuichi, was sent to South-East Asia and was never heard from again, but recently it came to light that he died in the fighting in Burma or somewhere. So, it has been decided that she shall now marry the younger brother. She is three years Ginzo's senior, you know. The villagers are calling it a happy event. Although, they do say that there will be hell to pay if it turns out that Yasuichi is still alive. This they add with a wry smile.

I thought this was all a little odd myself, but when I told Grandmother about it, she grew pensive.

'How old is Shinkichi now?' she said, seeming almost to ask herself the question.

Since there were just the two of us there, I replied, 'He's eight years older than me, so he must be twenty-five.'

'That's right,' she said. 'So, he's a year older than Rie...'

I looked at her in confusion, wondering what was going on. Realizing this, her face suddenly hardened, and she turned to me.

167

'Tsuruyo, you must never mention what I just said to anyone.'

Then, as if having made up her mind all of a sudden, she lit a candle in front of the Buddhist altar and stood before it with her hands pressed together in prayer for a long time.

I still have no idea what she must have been thinking.

3 JULY 1946

DAISUKE RETURNED STOP COME AT ONCE STOP MAKI

6 JULY 1946

How are you feeling now, Brother? Shikazo said that when he arrived at the sanatorium you had a fever and had come out in a rash again. Grandmother is very anxious to know how you are.

Try not to overexert yourself, Brother. If you get too worked up and your health, which until now has been getting better, worsens again, whatever should we do? Please spare a thought for your elderly grandmother, too. If the worst were to happen, then you would be all I had left.

But, oh, what a terrible shock! Recalling that day even now sends a chill straight to the pit of my stomach.

It was three days ago. I was in the storehouse, reading the book that you had sent me. In the next room, Grandmother had her glasses on and was doing some needlework. For the rainy season, it was a curiously cold evening, and it was drizzling on and off.

From time to time, I would look up from my book and glance over into the next room, where Grandmother was sitting, her hands neglecting the piece of cloth in her lap, her countenance lost in thought. It may be impertinent of me to say so, but I had a feeling that in that moment I knew exactly what was on her mind.

That afternoon, Ginzo had come with his new bride to pay their respects, you see. He had on, over his tanned body, a crested kimono that he had borrowed, and, whether because of the heat or because he felt embarrassed, he was perspiring heavily. But even so, he seemed to be in high spirits. His wife, Kanae, had plastered on a thick layer of white face powder, and she had even painted her hands white too, but, again, perhaps from embarrassment, despite being the elder by three years, she could not bring herself to look up. You know, her plump and rather sweet face makes her look younger, so the two of them do not look too mismatched. As you may remember, Ginzo had polio when he was little, and so one of his legs is a little lame (hence why he avoided the draft), but he is still strong enough and healthy enough to work as a farmer, in addition to being one of the most patient men in the village, so Kanae will surely be happy with him.

I overheard Rie and O-Sugi gossiping while the two of them were saying their goodbyes at the door.

'Kanae has such striking features, don't you think? When she puts on make-up like that, she's so beautiful that you could almost mistake her for somebody else,' Rie said. 'Just look how happy Ginzo seems…'

'But it's queer, isn't it, the younger brother marrying the older one's widow,' O-Sugi replied. 'And the groom being three years younger than the bride…'

'Oh, I doubt that matters much. What's important is that the two of them like each other.'

Rie said this very off-handedly, but then, hearing this, Grandmother weighed in.

'Well, that's one way of putting it. It's his late brother I feel sorry for,' she said, peering into Rie's face.

I am certain that this must have been what Grandmother was thinking about later that evening. Every now and then, I would hear a sigh escape her lips.

And that was when it happened. All of a sudden, we heard O-Sugi's frantic cries.

'Mistress! Oh, mistress, come quick! It's terrible! The young master…'

To begin with, I thought that you were the one she was talking about, Brother. I worried that perhaps your health had taken a turn for the worse. But I soon realized that I had been mistaken, for the next instant O-Sugi came bursting into the storehouse.

'Mistress,' she said to Grandmother, 'please come quick. The young master's come back to us, and he's brought a friend…'

I realized then that she had to be talking about Daisuke. I leapt to my feet and, without uttering a word, turned to look at Grandmother. All the colour had drained from her face: she looked as though she had been turned to stone.

Even now, I cannot explain her reaction. After all, Daisuke was always Grandmother's favourite. She would always turn a blind eye to his mischief and indulge him whenever she could. Because of this, she always found it very difficult to talk about him during the war, and she forever despaired at the prospect that something might happen to him. She would tell herself that he was dead, that he was not coming back, and she would secretly think about how she would cope if that were true. All this, however, was merely a result of her doting on Daisuke more than anyone else. And yet, why then, when the news arrived, did she look so pale and so grim?

Nevertheless, her colour soon improved. And then, as if having regretted hesitating a moment, she got to her feet.

'What's all this?' she said. 'Our Daisuke? Returned to us? Where is he?'

'He's in the vestibule, miss. With a friend.'

'Why haven't they come here? And where's Rie?'

'I've already told her, miss. But you'd better come right away.'

'Accompany me, please, Tsuruyo,' she said, turning to me.

Together we left the storehouse, passed along the dark corridor that led to the main house and then made our way to the vestibule. There, standing in that rectangular frame of the vestibule door, we saw two men in military uniform. They were both strangely quiet. Wondering what had happened to Rie, I looked around, but then I spotted her kneeling in a dim corner of the room, looking as if she might burst into tears at any moment. Hearing our footsteps, the figure standing nearest to us turned and stood stiffly to attention.

'Ah, you must be Mrs Honiden,' he said, addressing Grandmother. 'My name is Masaki. I've come to return Daisuke to you.'

'But… but what's wrong with him? Has something happened?' Her voice was trembling slightly. She was standing on her tiptoes, trying to see past the man blocking the doorframe.

'I regret to inform you that he's been injured… That's why I've had to accompany him… Daisuke, it's your grandmother.'

As he said this, the man stepped aside, and from behind him Daisuke took a few timid steps forward. That was the moment a chill ran through me.

Daisuke looked gaunt and haggard, and, to make matters worse, he had what looked like a large burn to his face. What unnerved me, though, was not the burn mark, but rather what I saw when Daisuke turned to me. Both his eyes were wide open, but neither of them moved. Even in that emotionally charged situation, they were completely devoid of expression. Whereas his lips and the muscles on his face showed signs of intense emotion, his eyes remained motionless and cold, as though he were completely indifferent. It was like looking into a gaping hole in his soul.

'Daisuke lost both his eyes in the war,' Masaki offered by way of explanation. 'That is why he has artificial eyes now.'

Listening to Masaki speak was almost like an out-of-body experience. It was as if he were talking about somebody else, somebody who had nothing to do with me. I stared past him and Daisuke, gazing out through the door into the open. A fine mizzle was falling from the dark sky, as usual, and suddenly a memory came rushing back to me. One rainy day Daisuke had returned home, and I remember thinking that his eyes did not look real. Such a silly thought…

Before I knew it, half a dozen villagers had gathered at the front gate and were looking at us. They were all whispering to each other and exchanging glances. Among them I spotted O-Rin. The rain was beading in fine droplets in her frizzy hair, but she, unfazed by this, was just peering timidly in through the gate.

I followed the line of O-Rin's intense gaze and, when I reached the end point, I was suddenly roused from my daydreaming. Her eyes were boring right into Daisuke's back.

THE VOTIVE TABLET

*On Tsuruyo's attempt to verify
Daisuke's identity*

12 JULY 1946

How have you been feeling since my last letter? Grandmother
was delighted by the news that the rash has gone. The temperature has suddenly shot up, though, so please remember
to take care of yourself.

Things here have also calmed down a little. The stream
of villagers who heard of Daisuke's return and came to visit
him has also dried up, and so the house is gradually returning to its usual quiet ways. Daisuke says that he is tired, so,
ever since his return, he has spent his time sleeping and
resting. He has been trying to avoid visitors, for the most
part, but the day before yesterday he did send for O-Rin
because he had to tell her about Goichi's last moments. Oh
yes, of course, I imagine you will not have heard. Apparently
Goichi Akizuki died in the war.

O-Rin kept us waiting quite a while, but she did come
in the end. Daisuke told her everything. Grandmother, Rie

174

and I were also there, listening. The following is, more or less, the story that he told.

During the fighting at Mengdao (?)—I did not quite catch the name—Daisuke and Goichi became separated from their unit. They were alone together, and, during an artillery bombardment, Goichi was hit and killed. Daisuke recovered a few of Goichi's personal effects, and, as he was wandering aimlessly by himself, he came under more artillery fire. He was hit by shrapnel and lost both of his eyes, and it was at that point that he collapsed. Fortunately, he was found by a friendly unit that happened to be passing by and was taken to safety.

'I don't know whether he had any last wishes,' Daisuke said, 'but I buried him myself, and this is what I retrieved from him.'

He produced a black, bloodstained notebook from his pocket. O-Rin had listened to the story in perfect silence, but even when it was over, she asked no questions. Truly, what a strange creature she is. Surely, under the circumstances, she might have been moved at least to shed a tear or two. And yet she just sat there, listening in silence, with a grim, almost angry look on her face. Even so, all the while she could not tear her eyes from Daisuke's face. She must have been upset that it was Daisuke who had come back alive and not Goichi. Come to think of it, perhaps it is only natural that I should feel sorry for her, too. That does not mean that I can find it in me to forgive her rudeness, though. For all

175

Daisuke's kindness in speaking to her, she just got up sullenly, without offering even a word of thanks, and left, taking the notebook with her.

But that was not all. Her behaviour had left Grandmother and Rie so stunned that it was I who had to rush after her to see her to the door. And it was there, in the dimly lit vestibule, that I spotted it: just when she thought no one was looking, a faint smile appeared on her lips.

Oh, that smile! For some reason, it sent a shiver right down my spine. It was so cruel and twisted as to defy description. The moment she sensed my presence, however, she stopped smiling and just glared at me menacingly before storming out.

I really do loathe that woman.

1 AUGUST 1946

I am sorry that I have not written in such a long while. I know I should write to you more often, but lately I have been so on edge. I cannot even put my finger on the reason for it, but, whatever it may be, I am scared. Yes, truly, I am frightened. I feel as though something terrible is in store. Oh, Brother, whatever should I do?

8 AUGUST 1946

Please forgive me, Brother. I really am sorry for causing you unnecessary worry by sending you that strange letter. Truth be told, I hesitated to send you this letter, as well. However, after that last one, I decided that I owe you an explanation, lest you worry even more, so here it is, in full. This is what has been troubling me lately. And please, Brother, you must tell me where I am going wrong.

Ever since Daisuke returned, everything in the house has been turned upside down. And not for the better. Things have changed drastically for the worse. In the old days, Daisuke was a cheery, compassionate, spirited man. Wherever he went, there was always laughter, and everybody he met could not help taking a shine to him.

But it is as if he were a different person now. Something has happened to him. Ever since he came back, his personality has been the exact opposite. I would not even call it melancholy. Rather, some dark cloud seems to have enveloped him. He has been back at home over a month now, but never once have I seen him smile.

Never mind smiling, he scarcely says a word. Whenever he needs something done, he just barks out an order. And he rarely talks. He prowls around the house like a cat, making no noise as he goes, and just listens intently, as though he were trying to sniff something out. Whenever I find him slowly walking down the corridor, dressed in his white *yukata*, his glass eyes glinting in the dim light as he stares blankly ahead, I feel a chill run down my spine.

I cannot escape those eyes. Even when I am reading a book or writing something in the storehouse, if I should suddenly remember those two lifeless pupils, I feel a steely coldness in my heart, as though a dagger has been pressed against it. I cannot shake the feeling that he is forever watching us with those glass eyes. And this is certainly not a delusion or some fixation of mine. No matter where in the house he is, he always knows exactly what is going on. He is watching us with those unseeing eyes, trying to find out what is being said between us, and what meaning is hidden between the words (even though there is no hidden meaning). What on earth can he be trying to find out?

The one I feel most sorry for is Rie. She is losing weight, although she tries to put it down to the summer heat causing her to lose her appetite. But I know for a fact that her dreadfully emaciated appearance cannot be explained away simply by a little warm weather.

Recently Grandmother has taken to whispering whenever she speaks to any member of the family. Only the other day she said to me, 'About Daisuke and Rie, Tsuruyo…'

'Yes?' I replied warily, staring at Grandmother's mouth.

I am sorry to say it, but she has aged rather rapidly in recent times. She seemed to hesitate a little, but, in the end, she came out with it.

'The two of them don't seem to be acting in the least like a married couple. Don't you think? They even sleep in separate beds! Childless at their age and sleeping in separate beds... It doesn't make sense to me.'

I blushed when she said this. I thought it was very improper of Grandmother to talk about that sort of thing. Let alone to someone of my age. But, come to think of it, maybe that was the point. What if the situation here is so grave that she felt unable to confide in anyone but me? What if I were the only person to whom she could unburden herself? Thinking this, I decided to listen quietly to what Grandmother had to say.

'But can't married couples sleep in separate beds? When Daisuke came back, he was exhausted. I think that's why he started sleeping by himself, and now it's become a habit.'

'Yes, it's not the sleeping in separate beds that bothers me so much as...' She paused. 'So much as the fact that they haven't... they haven't become man and wife again.'

'Oh!' I exclaimed, blushing now again. 'Grandmother, you mustn't say such things. But how do you know, anyway?'

'I just know. When you reach my age, you know a lot of things. But which one of them is at fault? There's no way that Daisuke would have gone off Rie. And besides, he's had to do without the company of women for quite some time.'

'But surely Rie hasn't gone off Daisuke?'

'Yes, that's why it's odd. I can't work it out. In any case, Daisuke seems like an entirely changed person.'

She sighed, seeming to resign herself to this. But when I heard those last words, a terrible shiver ran down my spine.

15 AUGUST 1946

I think you must have understood what I was hinting at in my previous letter, Brother. I received the letter you sent, reproaching me for even suspecting it. Of course it was an absurd idea. There is no way something like that could ever happen. It would be unthinkable.

But you must understand, Brother, that it is not only I who have such fears. Rie also harbours the exact same suspicion, although she is doing her best to hide it.

Yesterday I saw her just standing in the formal sitting room with a vacant expression on her face. She has lost so much weight this past month, as I mentioned before, so when I saw her standing there in that dimly lit room, she looked just like a ghost.

'What are you doing, Rie?' I asked, quietly approaching her from behind. I spoke in a soft voice so that nobody else would hear, but to her it seemed as if a bomb had gone off. She jumped and turned around.

When she saw that it was me, she smiled feebly and said, 'Oh, you gave me such a fright!'

'Sorry,' I said. 'I didn't mean to do that. But what are you doing here?'

180

'Me?' She tilted her head and stared at me intently, but then a smile flickered on her lips. 'I was just looking at the screen…'

Startled, I peered past her and saw that the Kuzunoha folding screen Grandmother had ordered to be taken out of the storehouse was still standing there. In the dusky light of the room, the painting seemed to glint mournfully, mirroring Rie.

'Oh? Is something wrong with it?' I asked, my eyes flitting between the two women. 'The screen, I mean…'

'Doesn't it strike you that this screen is a bad omen, Tsuruyo? Come on, the figure hasn't any eyes! Not unlike your brother…'

Her voice was trembling slightly.

'How did he lose his eyes?' she asked, almost talking to herself. 'And what were his eyes like before having those glass ones put in? Could it be…?'

'Rie!' I gasped aloud. But, even as I did, I tried to stifle the noise with my hands. 'Do you mean to say that…? Do you have a hunch about this? Have you noticed anything strange about Daisuke?'

Rie looked back at me in astonishment, her eyes bulging. They were so big that I thought I risked falling into them.

'Tsuruyo,' she said, taking my hand, 'I don't know what you're talking about. In any case, we must be careful about saying things before thinking, mustn't we? It isn't kind to say things about others just because we're finding it difficult. But still…' She let out another long, pained sigh. 'There's just something not right about this screen. It's tormenting me by stirring up all sorts of uninvited daydreams. This Kuzunoha is a *kitsune*, a fox-spirit. She isn't the real Princess Kuzunoha. But when this *kitsune* from the Forest of Shinoda took on the form of Princess Kuzunoha and went to bed with her husband, Abe no Yasuna, it was not out of malice. And besides, Yasuna was a man, so sleeping with another woman would hardly tarnish his honour. But what happens to a woman if the man she believed to be her husband turns out not to be her husband, but a perfect stranger. She would never be able to live with the shame…'

Do you understand now, Brother? There are others here who share my fears… Namely, Daisuke's wife, the one person who ought to know him best. But then, it is not just Rie and I who feel this way. Grandmother, too, has her doubts. Looking back on it all now, I think I can understand that look in O-Rin's eyes as she stood by the gate on the day when Daisuke returned. And then there was the time when Daisuke told her about Goichi's final moments: that uncanny smile she let slip when she was leaving. Had O-Rin already glimpsed the true identity of the man with the glass eyes before we did? Did she know then that this man was not in fact Daisuke but her own brother Goichi?

Brother, please help me! If this situation goes on much longer, I shall die. And before I do, Rie will either go mad or expire herself. I want to know for certain. Did the man

182

in our house really lose his eyes due to some injury? Or is it possibly the case that the only features distinguishing Daisuke and Goichi were gouged out on purpose? Could it be that it was not Goichi who was killed at Mengdao but Daisuke?

The idea is a horrible one! The thought alone is quite possibly driving me mad already. Oh, Brother, will you not tell me what to do? Is that man really Daisuke, or is he an impostor? How shall we ever be able to escape this never-ending hell until we know for sure?

23 AUGUST 1946

Thank you, Brother. You always have the answer. How could we have been blind to something so very simple?

Of course I remember the votive tablet. Before going off to war, departing soldiers would make their imprint on one and dedicate it to the guardian deity at the Onsaki Shrine in Okayama. It was believed that doing this would allow the soldiers to leave a part of themselves behind. Daisuke did the same before he left. I remember it as if it were yesterday: he imprinted his right hand on the wooden tablet and then Mr Shinden wrote the words FORTUNE IN BATTLE AND LONGEVITY on it.

The tablet must still be hanging in the shrine. It will be impossible to mistake, since Daisuke's name is written on the back of it. I do not know whether Goichi Akizuki dedicated a votive tablet himself, but what does it matter? So long as they still have Daisuke's, that alone will suffice.

I have read somewhere that everybody's fingerprints are different and that they never change. So even if Goichi never made a votive tablet, we shall surely be able to put an end to these terrible doubts, having just Daisuke's.

This evening I am going to ask O-Sugi to sneak out and go to the temple, and to find Daisuke's tablet and bring it back with her. Do not worry, though, Brother: I shall not tell her the real reason for this. I will find some excuse. How I wish I could go myself, but there is simply no way I could make the journey myself, what with that steep climb up to the shrine. And fear not: I shall not breathe a word of this to Rie or Grandmother, either. Not until things become clear…

Daisuke's fingerprints will dispel all doubts. Rest assured, I will not bungle it. I shall write again soon.

24 AUGUST 1946

Brother, help!

O-Sugi is dead. She fell from the cliff at the Onsaki Shrine. She went there, at my behest, to find the votive tablet. But she never came back.

This morning the Taguchi boy, Jitsuzo, reported that her body had been discovered at the foot of the cliff. Nobody knows that I had sent her there for the votive tablet, so people are beginning to wonder what on earth she was doing at the shrine.

I do not know what has become of the tablet. It may be still hanging there. Or perhaps O-Sugi found it and was pushed to her death while she was attempting to bring it back.

Brother, I am scared.

O-Sugi's funeral is set for the day after tomorrow. Please use that as an excuse to come back.

I think I am going mad.

A TERRIBLE TRAGEDY

On Tsuruyo's growing suspicions

29 AUGUST 1946

You must be exhausted, Brother. But even so, I cannot tell you how very much it cheered me to see you looking so unexpectedly well. Please, be sure to take good care of yourself. I want you back in this house by autumn, completely recovered. When you came back for the funeral, it struck me just how different this house feels with you in it.

Little by little, I am beginning to regain my presence of mind. You told me not to think too much, but that, I am afraid, is the one thing I cannot help but do. Until everything is resolved one way or another, all I can do is think. How I wanted to talk it all over with you when you were here, Brother, but there were so many people around, making it impossible. Lately, my thoughts are all I have had.

You may chide me for saying what I am about to say, but if I keep silent, I shall get angry and bitter. And there is nobody for me to talk to but you. Do not be too harsh on me, Brother. Please, indulge my rambling thoughts.

Can O-Sugi's fall from that cliff really have been an accident? No, that would be too terrible a coincidence. I can only think that someone pushed her. But who? And why? I do not have an answer to the first question, but I think I know the answer to the second one. O-Sugi was murdered because of that votive tablet. Which means that her killer must have wanted to stop her getting her hands on it. But why were they so determined to do so? The answer to that is so obvious that it needs hardly be stated. Whoever it was did not want the handprint on that tablet to be compared with the hand of the man with the glass eyes in our house. In other words, that person with the glass eyes is not our brother, Daisuke. It has to be Goichi Akizuki, after all.

You always accuse me of being too rational and getting carried away with games of logic, Brother, so I try to restrain myself as much as possible, but in this case I cannot. This is no game. This is a matter of life and death.

So, when I put it like that, you can surely see who would have had most to lose if the votive tablet were to have fallen into O-Sugi's hands. Why, it would be the very man with the glass eyes, who right now is playing the part of Daisuke. He would know exactly what the importance of that votive tablet was and why O-Sugi was on her way to fetch it.

I told you in a previous letter that he knows everything that is said in this house. He must have overheard me ask

O-Sugi to go and get it. He must have understood what was going on immediately. The only trouble is that he is blind. Even if he had the will to follow O-Sugi and kill her, it would have been impossible for him to carry out. A man who has suddenly lost his sight cannot simply venture out without a guide.

And yet…

Having got this far, something occurs to me. Yes… The day before O-Sugi died, or, to be more precise, the evening after I asked her to undertake this task for me, I saw him in the back garden, talking to somebody over the hedgerow. They were speaking in low, hushed tones, so I could not tell what the subject of their discussion was, but, when I realized that this other person was none other than O-Rin, I recall being overcome by a strange, indescribable wave of apprehension.

That must have been it. He must have asked O-Rin to kill O-Sugi.

And, thinking about it, when he said goodbye to her and turned to make his way back to the house, there was such a terrible look on his face that defied description…

Oh, the horror of it!

It must have been O-Rin who pushed O-Sugi to her death. She must be conspiring with Goichi to take over this house. Once, when I was little, somebody told me that O-Rin's father threw himself down a well because he hated Father so very much, and that her mother followed suit only a year after. The two siblings must be trying to avenge their parents. But what can we do? We are powerless. Please, you must do something, Brother. You are our only hope.

I wonder what became of the all-important votive tablet…

30 AUGUST 1946

Two awful things happened between last night and this morning.

The first was that there was a break-in at around midnight. It was I who noticed it. Ordinarily, Grandmother is a very alert woman, but lately she has been showing her age and dozing off more and more, even in the afternoon. Hence, I was the first to wake up when it happened.

I was having a bad dream at the time. I dreamt that Kuzunoha had stepped out of the painted screen, but before I knew it she had transformed into Daisuke and was staring back at me with those eerie glass eyes.

I awoke with a jolt, but then I heard a noise, like someone forcing open one of the storm shutters. At first, I thought it must be a mouse gnawing on something, but the very next moment I heard the rattle of a storm shutter again, and I leapt out of bed.

'Grandmother! Grandmother!'

I called out to the next room, but there was no reply. All I could hear was the regular, even respiration of her slumber.

Although I was afraid, I opened the sliding door, crept into Grandmother's room and tried to rouse her. Fortunately, she woke up right away.

'Grandmother, I heard a strange noise,' I whispered in her ear before she could say a word. 'I think it came from the main house…'

Startled, she sat up in her bed.

'A strange noise? What kind of a noise?'

'It sounded like someone forcing one of the storm shutters open. I'm sure it was coming from the tatami room.'

Grandmother pricked up her ears and listened intently, but she did not hear anything out of the ordinary.

'It'll just be mice, Tsuruyo.'

'No, it wasn't. I thought that myself at first, but it definitely sounded like somebody opening one of the storm shutters.'

'Well, we'd better go and take a look,' Grandmother said after a pause.

Although her health has been declining recently, she is still the same resolute woman she has always been. After quickly tying her obi, she gently opened the sliding door. I was still afraid, but to be left behind alone was an even more frightening prospect, so I hurried after her.

We walked along the roofed corridor that links the storehouse to the main house, and I spotted that one of the storm shutters by the lavatory was lying open. I gripped Grandmother's hand, my heart pounding. What an incredible woman she is. Any ordinary person in her situation would have raised the alarm at once, but she, on the contrary, tiptoed over to the *shoji* leading to the formal sitting room and peered in through one of the glass panels in the sliding door. I followed her lead.

Naturally, the lights in the room were turned off. However, one storm shutter and one *shoji* door were open, so we could make out the vague outlines of things in the pale moonlight that was streaming in. You already know, Brother, that this is the room where Grandmother had put the Kuzunoha folding screen. And there, right in front it, was a figure. We could not see who it was, of course, but, judging by the vague silhouette, it looked like a young man. Curiously enough, he was just standing there, staring at the screen, seemingly without a care in the world. He seemed to be transfixed by it, as though Kuzunoha herself had bewitched him.

'Who is that?' Grandmother suddenly asked. She whispered, but her voice was sharp, and it carried.

Hearing this, the man span around and dashed through the gap in the open *shoji* out onto the veranda, and then into the dark. He was in such a hurry, though, that he banged his shin on the low dining table. It made such a terrific noise. He must have really hurt himself, but he looked so funny limping as he tried to run off.

All this commotion appeared to wake Daisuke and Rie, who had been asleep in the next room. There was a click, and light began streaming in through the gaps in the transom, and, before long, Rie appeared, opening one of the *fusuma* sliding doors.

'Oh, it's you, Grandmother,' she said. 'What was all that noise just now?'

'It was a burglar!'

'A burglar?'

'Yes, he broke in by forcing one of the storm shutters. Tsuruyo woke up just in time, so I don't think he's managed to take anything… Tsuruyo, turn the light on.'

When I turned on the light, I could see a trail of muddy footprints leading from the veranda to the screen, but nothing else seemed to be amiss.

'How odd,' said Rie. 'I didn't hear a thing.'

'You have to be more careful,' said Grandmother. 'He must have been listening to your breathing while you slept.'

'What a ghastly thought.'

'It's all right now, though. He went running out again. I doubt he'll come back. Lock all the doors tightly and go back to sleep.'

Oddly enough, throughout all this commotion, Daisuke did not even bother to get up. And yet he was not asleep. When I peered through the gap in the *fusuma*, I saw him sitting up in bed, listening intently to our conversation. Even behind the gently billowing white mosquito net, I could see those eerie glass eyes of his staring back at me… Their two beds were arranged side by side.

That was the first incident that happened last night; the second one happened not half an hour later.

After the commotion with the burglar had come to an end, Grandmother and I returned to the storehouse, but I was so agitated that I could not sleep at all. Then, as I lay there tossing and turning, I heard yet another strange noise. Once again, it was coming from the main house, and it sounded like somebody's stifled groaning. Startled, I sat up in bed. Hearing it, too, Grandmother called out to me from the next room.

'Tsuruyo, can you hear that voice, too?'

'Yes, Grandmother. What do you think it is? Do you suppose the robber has come back?'

'Let's go and find out.'

We made our way back over to the main house. There was nothing wrong with the storm shutters this time; the groaning was coming from Daisuke's bedroom on the far side of the formal sitting room. I gently slid open the *shoji*. There was a light on in the bedroom, which was shining through the gaps in the transom and projecting its carved pattern of clouds onto the ceiling. It sounded as though the groaning was coming from Rie.

'Daisuke? Rie? What's going on? Is anything the matter?' said Grandmother, pressing her sleeve to her mouth so as not to speak too loudly.

But no answer came from the bedroom. The only sound was that of Rie's stifled groaning. Or rather, no—it was mixed with the sound of Daisuke's heavy breathing and the occasional muffled profanity.

Grandmother was understandably hesitant, but the situation was too odd for her to abandon it now. She placed her hand to the sliding door and gently opened it a fraction so that she could see inside. I, too, peered inside from under Grandmother's sleeve, but what I saw was so terrible that I felt as though a lead weight had been placed in the pit of my stomach.

There, inside the mosquito netting, was Rie, stripped to the waist, lying face-down and pinned to the ground under the weight of Daisuke. He was twisting her arm back so violently that it looked as though it might break at any moment, and, with the palm of his other hand, he was feeling the right side of her torso. In that moment, his face was like that of a demon from hell. Oh, what an appalling sight it was! Truly, it was indescribable.

'Daisuke!' Grandmother could not help shouting. 'What ever are you doing?'

Thus alerted to our presence, Daisuke suddenly jumped off of Rie.

'I'm blind! I can't see anything!' he shouted and began tearing at his hair with both hands.

Rie lay there, as though lifeless. Her long hair, having come undone, trailed along the white sheets like a snake, moving every time she was convulsed by sobs. She continued sobbing for quite some time.

Will you not tell me what is going on, Brother? When she got up this morning, Rie looked ashen-faced, but no matter how Grandmother asks, she refuses to say what transpired last night. Daisuke, meanwhile, has shut himself away in the bedroom and refuses to come out.

Could there be some connection between this and the burglary last night? And if so, who was the burglar? I simply do not understand. I do not understand a thing. The only thing I do know is that something terrible is going to happen. But what?

2 SEPTEMBER 1946

I do not know quite how to tell you this, Brother, but Rie has been killed. Daisuke is nowhere to be found, and the shock of it has caused Grandmother to collapse and slip into a coma.

I have given this letter to Shikazo to deliver. Have him bring you here on his bicycle. You must come at once. Please.

THE TRUTH, AS REPORTED IN THE NEWSPAPERS

On successive reversals of suspicion

Newspaper clipping dated 3 September 1946

MURDER AMID A STORM

Victim Is Wife of Wealthy Family

Yesterday, in the early hours, a terrible murder was discovered amid a violent storm. The victim was one Rie (24), wife of Daisuke Honiden, a wealthy landowner from K—— (a village in K—— District). The deceased was discovered hacked to pieces in her bedroom. She was discovered by her sister-in-law, Tsuruyo Honiden (17). According to an announcement made by officials who raced to the scene, the murder is believed to have been committed at around midnight. Curiously, the whereabouts of the victim's husband, Daisuke Honiden (28), are unknown. The husband is a war veteran who served in the Southern theatre and was demobbed in July of this year; he was blinded during the war and cannot set foot outside without assistance. In addition to these three, the household further includes a grandmother, Maki (78), and a manservant, Shikazo. None of them became aware of the tragedy until morning, however, because the previous night's howling winds and driving rain muffled the sound of screams.

Newspaper clipping dated 4 September 1946

HUSBAND FOUND IN WELL
Bloody Handprint Found on Folding Screen

Previously this newspaper reported that a search was under way for Daisuke Honiden, the missing head of the wealthy family at the heart of the murder case that has shocked the village of K——. His body was discovered unexpectedly on the night of the 2nd and dragged from a well in the back garden of the family property. It is believed that Mr Honiden was thrown into the well after having his heart gouged out. The murder weapon has not yet been found. Furthermore, a bloody handprint that appears to have been left by the perpetrator was found on a treasured folding screen in the room next to the bedroom where the crime was committed. If this is indeed the perpetrator's handprint, it is expected that the case will be solved in double-quick time. The police have already launched a major manhunt.

WAS IT ONE OF THEM?

The Complex Politics of the Honiden Family

There has been a sudden change of direction in the ongoing police investigation into the Honiden murder case in the village of K——. The police have identified the bloody handprint left behind on the folding screen as belonging to the victim, Daisuke Honiden. Additionally, a desperate search conducted by the police has led to the discovery of a sword made by the renowned swordsmith Hikoshiro Sadamune in the long grass to the rear of the Honiden mansion. This blade is believed to be the murder weapon, although it is the property of the family and was displayed in the *tokonoma* alcove of the formal reception room. None of the family members can recall when the sword went missing; however, these developments would appear to suggest that the perpetrator may in fact be a member of the Honiden household itself. The police are taking all this into account, and the family members have been questioned, but so far no conclusive evidence has emerged. One person of particular interest is the victim's younger brother, Shinkichi Honiden (25), who has been for some time in the care of the H—— Sanatorium, situated 15 miles from the village of K——, and who seemingly returned to the family home the day after the incident took place, having received a communiqué from his younger sister, Miss Tsuruyo Honiden. This was investigated thoroughly by the police, and his alibi for the night in question has been verified. There have also been questions raised about the fact that the man-servant, Shikazo, was discovered on the morning of the 2nd soaked to the skin and with his bicycle covered in mud; this was explained, however, by his having been dispatched to the sanatorium by Miss Honiden immediately after the incident was discovered, braving wind and rain to fetch her brother. There are also rumours that, while Daisuke's fate remained uncertain before he was demobbed, the old matron of the house intended to have Rie marry Shinkichi in the event that Daisuke did not return from the war, and that this may have been the motive for the crime.

Newspaper clipping dated 6 September 1946

WAS IT REALLY DAISUKE?

Bizarre Revelations in the Honiden Case

Another bizarre twist has been uncovered in the Honiden double-murder case. This following statement was made by Rin Akizuki (35), a resident in the village of K——:

'The victim wasn't Daisuke. It was my younger brother,

Goichi Akizuki. Everybody in the village knows that Daisuke and Goichi were the spitting image of one another. Just look at this photograph of them taken during the war. You can't tell them apart, can you? The only difference between them was that Goichi suffered from polycoria, a condition that meant he had twin pupils in both eyes, while Daisuke didn't. So, when Daisuke was killed in battle, Goichi gouged his own eyes out and stole Daisuke's identity. He did this so that he could take revenge on the Honiden family because he had been so ill-treated by them, despite being the illegitimate son of Daizaburo Honiden, the previous head of the family. Who was it that killed him, then? It hardly needs to be spelt out. It was the whole lot of them. Just look at Shinkichi's movements on the night in question. I'm sure he must have sneaked out of the sanatorium and made the journey to the village. Five hours would have been enough to get there and back by bicycle. He must have slipped out, killed my brother and thrown his body down the well before creeping back to the sanatorium before daylight. Killing Rie was probably just an added bonus, or perhaps she caught him in the act...' etc., etc.

The investigation has revealed, however, that Rin's accusations are unfounded. As has been reported previously, Mr Shinkichi Honiden has an established alibi. Two of the night duty nurses at the sanatorium have attested that at no point could Mr Honiden have left the sanatorium for longer than two hours, let alone five. The duty nurses make their rounds of the patients' bedrooms every hour or two, and Mr Honiden takes sleeping pills to help him sleep at night.

There is, furthermore, a curious piece of evidence that has come to light regarding the all-important eyes of the victim, on which Rin's story depended. The victim had artificial glass eyes; however, when the body was recovered, the right eye was found to be missing. Despite a painstaking search of the Honiden property, it has still not been recovered. Where is this artificial eye? Could it be the key to solving this mystery?

Newspaper clipping dated 7 September 1946

WAS IT AN EX-CON?
Back to Square One for the Honiden Case

A new suspect has emerged in the Honiden murder case that is hanging over the village of K——. The suspect is one Shoji Ono (25), the eldest son of Uichiro Ono (64), who was evacuated to the village during the war. Young Mr Ono has three previous convictions, and on 6 June this year he escaped from the prison where he was being held under an assumed name. The police had been on the lookout for him since his escape, believing that he might be staying with his parents, but a witness has come forward, claiming to have spotted him in the local area in the early hours of 2 September. There is also a report that the Honiden residence was broken into four days prior to the tragedy, late on the night of 29 August, so suspicion for the burglary has also fallen on Mr Ono. It is believed that the Ono family harbours a deep grudge against the Honiden family. Police have launched a search for the man in question.

Newspaper clipping dated 10 September 1946

AN ARREST IN THE HONIDEN CASE!
Suspect Had the Artificial Eye in His Pocket

Shoji Ono, who was wanted for questioning in connection with the Honiden murder case, has been arrested while hiding out at the house of an acquaintance in the city of O——. As soon as Mr Ono was taken into custody by the police, a body search revealed that he was in possession of an artificial eye. The glass prosthetic was found in Mr Ono's jacket pocket, raising the alarm. It is believed that the eye must have become dislodged while the body was being transported to the well, falling into Mr Ono's pocket. If it can be established that this is indeed the missing eye, it is expected that the suspect will make a full confession, and the case will soon be closed.

Newspaper clipping dated 12 September 1946

ONO CONFESSES!
The Real Story of the Grisly Crime

Shoji Ono (25), who was arrested as the prime suspect in the Honiden case, confessed last night to the double murder. The following, based on his statement, outlines the grisly details of the incident.

The Ono family was once, together with the Honidens, one of the most prominent families in the village of K——. However, owing to the shrewdness of the former head of the Honiden family, Daizaburo, and to that of his predecessor, Shojiro, the Ono family was stripped of its assets and was forced of necessity to leave the village for Kobe. After 30 successful years in the city, the war left the family destitute once again and forced them to return to the village, where they were regarded as failures and shunned by the locals. With so many mouths to feed, the Ono family was barely able to make ends meet, so they sought the return of a valuable folding screen, a family heirloom that had been entrusted to the Honiden family for safekeeping some 30 years previously, but the Honiden family refused to return it. Then, after Mr Ono broke out of prison, he returned to his father's house in the village, where he learnt of all this and became so enraged by it that he resolved to kill the entire Honiden family.

The details of the crime itself were given as follows. On the night of 29 August, he made his first attempt on the Honiden family, but he was caught by a member of the household and fled in a panic. He was, however, able to abscond with the Sadamune blade. Later, on the night of 1 September, under cover of a storm that was raging, Mr Ono sneaked back into Honiden residence, where he made his way to the bedroom of Mr Daisuke Honiden and his wife, now having a sound knowledge of the layout from his previous visit. He first killed Mrs Honiden, hacking her to pieces while she slept. Awoken by the noise and surprised by the smell of blood in the air, the blind Mr Honiden then leapt out from under the mosquito net, ran into the next room and past the folding screen, after which Mr Ono stabbed him and gouged out his heart. Crazed with bloodlust, Mr Ono then proceeded to search for other members of the Honiden family, but fortunately Mr Honiden's mother and younger sister were sound asleep in the storehouse and thus narrowly escaped this danger. As soon as Mr Ono realized that he was not going to be able to find them, he threw Mr Honiden's corpse down the well and flung the murder weapon into the long grass before fleeing the scene, but little did he know that his victim's glass eye had fallen into his pocket. Such are the grisly details of the Honiden murder case.

A FORMIDABLE SISTER

On Tsuruyo's truth

7 OCTOBER 1946

It feels odd to be writing to you, dear Brother, now that we live under the same roof again, but lately my mind has been in such turmoil, so today I wanted to sit down and put my thoughts in order while I still have the strength left in me. I could think of no other way to do this, and I know, moreover, that if I do not do this now, then it will soon be too late. Ever since Daisuke returned to us, my heart has been wracked by suspicion, tension and dread, and, when the tragedy came to pass, I thought it would stop beating in an instant. The only thing that kept me going was my sense of responsibility. After Grandmother collapsed, I had no choice but to remain strong. Knowing this held my fragile life together, but even that has its limits. The unexpected discovery I made only a few days ago has dealt me such a terrible, crushing blow that I doubt I shall be able to go on living much longer.

What was this discovery? Well may you ask. The day before yesterday, I was sitting at Grandmother's bedside, pouring out my all my incoherent thoughts and feelings of despondency, as she just lay there unconscious. You were not at home, having gone out somewhere, and Shikazo was out in the fields. I was alone, staring out of the window at the dazzling red of the amaranth in the garden. And that was when I noticed. There was something not quite right about the tatami mat on which I was sitting. I paid little attention to it at first. I changed position a couple of times, but no matter which way I sat, I just could not get comfortable. When I glanced down at the tatami mat, I saw that the edge was sticking up a little. I thought this was quite strange: Grandmother was so fastidious that she would never have tolerated the mats not being fitted together properly. There had to be something stuck under the mat. But *what*?

I lifted up the edge of the tatami mat and saw something lying there underneath it wrapped in *hosho* paper. I felt an odd sense of foreboding. What could be hidden in a place like that?

I looked over at Grandmother and saw that she was sound asleep. I felt guilty, but curiosity got the better of me. Ever so quietly I picked up the package from under the mat. It was hard to the touch, like a little board, and it immediately reminded me of something. I hurriedly removed the wrapping paper.

Just as I feared, it was a votive tablet. And what is more, it was the one that Daisuke offered at the Onsaki Shrine before going off to war, and the one that O-Sugi lost her life trying to retrieve.

Imagine my surprise, Brother! Even now, the very memory of finding it there makes my heart skip a beat. What on earth was Grandmother doing with that votive tablet? After all, it was in her room, and I could tell by the wrapping that it was her hand that had done it. So, she must have been the one who put it there. But what was she doing with it in the first place? The answer to that question struck such fear into me that I wanted to cry out loud.

Since I made this discovery, I have been thinking about it night and day. As you know, Brother, I cannot rest once I have the bit between my teeth—not until things are resolved one way or another. I kept turning it over and over in my mind. Then, after much thought, I reached the following conclusion.

I cannot imagine Grandmother having pushed O-Sugi to her death. For the last few years, she has had difficulty walking and rarely ventures outside, so it is inconceivable that she could have climbed the steep hill up to the shrine. Could she have asked someone else to go and fetch the votive tablet for her? Yet in that case, she must have known the significance of the tablet. But however clever she might have been, that seems unlikely. And I doubt that there is anybody whom she would trust enough to carry out the task. Except for you alone, Brother…

Having reached this point in my thinking, it suddenly dawned on me. It was you who fetched the votive tablet. But when did you bring it here? That was when I remembered: you came home from the sanatorium just after O-Sugi died. Her fall from the cliff must have come as a shock to you. It must have made you wonder what had really happened. Did you then go to the shrine yourself in secret and find the votive tablet hanging right where it ought to be? Was it then that you realized O-Sugi's death had absolutely nothing to do with the tablet and must have been a simple accident?

It must have been. Now I realize my terrible mistake. What a fool I have been! I built for myself this imaginary tower of dread and cowered in fear of its shadow. This is immediately apparent from a comparison of the imprint on the votive tablet with the bloody handprint left on the folding screen. They are an exact match. And the police also said that the handprint on the screen was a match for that of the body recovered from the well. In other words, the man with the glass eyes was our brother, after all. It really was Daisuke…

What kind of a sister have I been? Suspecting my own brother of being someone else, spying on him, whispering about him behind his back, compounding his loneliness and his misfortune…

What a foolish, wicked person I have been! But why, Brother, did you not tell me about the votive tablet? I think I can guess the reason. Knowing that the presence of the votive tablet at the shrine would confirm the identity of the man with the glass eyes one way or another, you did not want to risk burdening a delicate young woman like me with this dangerous and important task. And so, instead, you told Grandmother in secret. She was keeping it hidden so that she could compare Daisuke's prints whenever the opportunity arose. And yet… when that opportunity did eventually present itself, Daisuke was already dead.

Thus, the questions regarding the votive tablet have been solved. It is now time to address those terrible murders.

Shoji Ono confessed to the murders, but I have always known this to be an untruth. I knew this not only in my gut, but also from a logical standpoint: there were some things that simply did not stack up. Shoji claimed to have taken the Sadamune sword when he broke in on the night of the 29th of August, but I distinctly recall seeing it in the formal sitting room on the night of the 1st of September. Shoji is therefore lying. He must have been volunteering to take on the role of perpetrator in order to protect someone. But who? Who was the real culprit?

I scoured the newspapers from around the time of the tragedy once again and drew the following conclusion. The police at the time were keeping a very close eye on you, Brother, but in the end, they let you off because you had a perfect alibi. You definitely could not have made the thirty-mile journey there and back in a single evening; consequently, you could not be involved in the murder case… So ran their reasoning.

But I have been thinking about this. Is it really impossible that you could be guilty? Fifteen miles separate the H—— Sanatorium from the village of K——. Given the time it takes to travel that distance by bicycle, and the testimony of your nurses, the distance seems to provide you with an unshakeable alibi. And yet it does not. You see, there are two possible ways you could have committed murder. One is that you went to the victim; the second is that the victim came to you. Your alibi means the former was impossible. But as for the latter…

What an enormous oversight on the part of the police not to consider this eventuality. The fact that the victim was blind and could not venture out without an escort seemed to blind the police themselves to the notion that it *would* be possible for him to go out, so long as he had an escort. And if somebody—Shikazo, for instance—were to give him a lift on his bicycle, it would be quite possible to get to the sanatorium from K——. It is also quite possible, furthermore, that you met him in the environs of the sanatorium, killed him, and had Shikazo dispose of the body in the well.

There is a reason that I have come to such a terrible conclusion, Brother. In fact, there are three reasons for it.

The first is that when Shikazo discovered Rie's body and, in his surprise, went up to the storehouse to wake us, the clothes he had been wearing were sopping wet and had been hung up to dry, and his bicycle was covered in mud. The police noticed this as well, but they decided that he must have got drenched when he went to pick you up at the sanatorium—which he did before the police arrived. I purposely turned a blind eye to this.

The second is that Rie was killed at around midnight on the night of the 1st to the 2nd of September, but I distinctly heard the well wheel creaking at around five o'clock the following morning. There is no doubt in my mind that that was when Daisuke was thrown into the well. But that made me wonder why the perpetrator had to wait from midnight until dawn.

The third reason is the fact that Rie's body was left lying in the tatami room, whereas Daisuke's body had been thrown down the well. There had to be a good reason for this. Namely, that Daisuke had got soaked on his way to the sanatorium and his body had got covered in mud on the way back, so he could not be left in the tatami room.

I can see the scene that night in my mind's eye right now, Brother. Daisuke had been informed by O-Rin that there was an illicit relationship going on between you and Rie. And that night, in a jealous rage, Daisuke hacked the young lady to shreds and forced Shikazo to take him to the H—— Sanatorium, where he tried to kill you. Only, you ended up killing Daisuke. You then had Shikazo put the body on his bicycle again and take it back to the house around dawn, whereupon he threw the body into the well.

Looking up at the sky from the storehouse window after writing all this, I see clouds floating in the clear blue heavens, like clumps of sheep's wool. As I gaze at these clouds, I feel as though my body itself is floating in the air, and that I am about to drift up to heaven. It is as if all my pain and sorrow have been sublimated, and my body has become transparent like glass.

I do not know why Shoji Ono volunteered to play the role of the murderer. But the two of you were once awfully close friends, if I am not mistaken. I would never dream of questioning Shikazo in an attempt to have my suspicions confirmed. I would prefer simply to remain in the dark and then, when the time comes, to disappear into the unknown like a gust of wind.

And that time, I fear, is nigh. Farewell, Brother. I have failed as a sister.

SHINKICHI'S POSTSCRIPT

8 DECEMBER 1946

She was a formidable girl, my sister.

Since Tsuruyo's last letter describes everything about the incident, sparing no detail, what more is there for me to add? I should, however, like to record briefly the anguish that my brother felt leading up to the incident as well as the circumstances of the incident itself.

Never would I have dreamt that my brother was wracked by such terrible suspicions. Until he came to kill me that night and hurled all those crazed epithets at me, I had no idea of the awful secret that was burdening his heart.

When Goichi died, Daisuke was the only person there to comfort him. Apparently, as he lay there in the throes of death, he told my brother, 'Your wife, Rie, and I were once together. If you don't believe me, check the right side of her lower abdomen, by her groin, next time you see her. She has a little birthmark shaped like a gourd. Knowing this is my proof that she gave herself to me.'

Although my brother had been married to his wife for just under a year, he was a man of great moderation and restraint and did not yet know every inch of that woman's body. Hence, Goichi's confession not only astonished him, but also threw him into a morass of suspicion. What is more, Daisuke was blinded soon after this, and so the fact that he was unable to verify this story became a kind of living hell for him.

This was in fact the cause of that dark aura that shrouded him when he returned from the war. To make matters worse, O-Rin then instilled in him the idea of his wife's infidelity with his younger brother, plunging him into the depths of despair. Shaken by what Goichi had told him, he was now in the perfect state of mind to believe O-Rin's baseless slander. But then something else happened to compound his misfortune.

On the night of the 29th of August, somebody stole into the room beside Daisuke's bedroom. As the police have confirmed, this was Shoji Ono, but Daisuke mistakenly believed that it was me. My grandmother and my younger sister both knew this, but they did not tell me because they thought they were protecting me. How agonizing the suspicions of a blind man must be! My brother, moreover, never voiced his misgivings, and this forbidding silence only made us fear him more, which in turn caused his doubts to fester.

On the night of the storm, my brother's resentment, which he had suppressed until then, suddenly exploded. In a jealous rage, he killed Rie, slashing her to pieces, before threatening Shikazo with the bloody murder weapon and forcing the servant to take him to the H—— Sanatorium.

As everybody knows, sanatoriums for tuberculosis patients are built in a very open style. The ward I am in is located at the very rear of the building, so it is possible to reach it via a corridor at the back. Shikazo had visited me many times before, so he knew the way to my room well.

Never I shall forget that night. At around two o'clock in the morning, I was awoken by Shikazo, who then led me out into the hills behind the sanatorium, where I found, to my astonishment, my brother waiting for me. Daisuke ordered Shikazo to leave at once, and then, for the first time, he accused me of betrayal. I had no idea about what Goichi had told him, but, as far as I was concerned, I was innocent, and so of course I protested as much. But Daisuke was no longer listening. He suddenly drew a sword and lunged at me.

I have no inclination to talk about what happened next. Or rather, even if I did want to talk about it, I am not sure that I could, so jumbled are my memories. We struggled while the storm raged about us. I put up a fight, wanting only to save myself and bring my brother back to his senses. We fell to the ground while we were grappling with each other, but after that my brother stopped moving. When I

215

came to my senses, I saw that the sword had been plunged all the way to the hilt into my brother's chest. Curiously, there was not a single drop of blood.

I do not recall whether I considered having the body transported to K—— and dumped in the well, but I do remember immediately calling Shikazo over and showing him what was left of Daisuke. Horrified by the sight of it, he began to tremble with fear, but then said something along the following lines: 'He would've had to die sooner or later, Master Shinkichi. He's just killed his wife, you see. Why don't I take the body back on my bicycle? That way, nobody will be any the wiser that he came here…'

Shikazo's words gave me the inspiration for the plan that I then hatched. Daisuke's body had to be thrown down the well for the very reason that Tsuruyo deduced. I had wanted to keep the two bodies together, but there was simply no way that I could leave a soaking wet body in the tatami room. Little could I imagine then, however, that my plan would work so well, or that Shikazo's lips would remain so tightly sealed. All I wanted in that moment was to give myself enough distance from the incident that I could put my thoughts in order.

Shoji took responsibility for my crime for the reason that Tsuruyo guessed. Throughout the four years of his childhood that he spent in K——, he and I were the best of friends. So, after he was demobbed and turned out of

216

his own home by O-Saki, he came to see me at the sanatorium. I gave him a little money, and, from then on, he would sometimes visit me in secret. After he escaped from the prison in O——, I was his first port of call. I had no intention of going against the law, but I had always felt a little sorry for Shoji. In no way did I agree with the path he had trodden in recent times, but still I sympathized with him because he had had so little choice in the matter. That is why, far from reporting him, I tried to help him out, in whatever way I could.

On the night in question, Shoji had also come to see me. After I had dispatched Shikazo, I woke Shoji up and told him the whole story. He seemed surprised but, without even blinking, he said to me, 'Don't worry, Shinkichi. If it comes down to it, you can pin the lot of it on me. You and I have both made mistakes. And besides, what difference does it make whether I take the blame for one or for two murders?'

Shoji laughed darkly as he said all this.

He then left to check whether any evidence had been left behind, and soon he came back with a grin on his face.

'What did I just say about making mistakes?' he said. 'Look here. Could there be a more perfect piece of evidence?'

That was when he produced Daisuke's glass eye in the palm of his hand. I distinctly remember a blood-curdling chill running through me the moment I saw it.

'I'd better take this,' he said. 'That way, there'll be no doubt that it was me.'

Shortly after that, Shoji left the sanatorium, making sure that people spotted him in the local area.

I think I have said all that I intended to say. Or, no—there is one more important thing that I have to impart. When I came to the house at Tsuruyo's behest on the morning of the 2nd, the first thing I did was to check Rie's body. She had no birthmark anywhere. Such was the revenge of the Akizuki siblings. Ah, my poor brother…

Tsuruyo died on the 15th of October. A girl with a heart as weak and a mind as sharp as hers was never long for this world. Perhaps this was for the best. Grandmother also passed away a week ago. I did not tell her anything, although I suspect she must have known at least part of the matter. And so now, the only surviving member of the Honiden family is the one writing this postscript.

Once I have finished writing it, I intend to send it, along with a bundle of Tsuruyo's letters, to Kosuke Kindaichi.

Kosuke Kindaichi… I had heard this name from the famous murders on Gokumon Island. And when I learnt that he had somehow become involved in a reinvestigation of this case, I was both surprised and afraid.

I had no intention of running away. My only concern was Grandmother. Having lost my brother and his wife, and then Tsuruyo, I was the only one on whom she could depend.

Then one day, Kosuke Kindaichi finally paid me a visit. We exchanged only a few words, but from those alone I could tell that he had figured out the truth of what had gone on here. Having already resigned myself to my fate, I handed over my sister's final letter in silence.

The detective glanced at the letter in puzzlement, but, as he read on, a look of profound astonishment spread over his face. Having reached the end, he stared blankly into the distance for a few moments, before eventually returning his gaze to me.

'Well…' he muttered, his eyes glinting darkly.

'Well…' I parroted back, unable to find the words to continue.

Kosuke Kindaichi's eyes bored into me, but then his face suddenly broke into a smile.

'Anyway, how is your grandmother getting on?' he asked.

'It won't be long now,' I replied. 'I doubt she'll see in the new year.'

'I see, I see…' he muttered indistinctly, before turning his misty eyes to me.

'I think it would be best not to show this letter to anyone else for the time being. At least, not until your grandmother's time has come… I'm sorry to have barged in on you like this.'

And with that, the detective left just as breezily as he arrived.

Kosuke Kindaichi extracted no promises from me, and neither did I offer any. Yet my honour must be preserved. Now that I have bid my grandmother farewell, I no longer have any cause for regret. After dispatching these letters at the post office, I shall take the only path that is open to me...

COMING SOON FROM PUSHKIN VERTIGO

Seishi Yokomizo

SHE WALKS AT NIGHT

AVAILABLE AND COMING SOON
FROM PUSHKIN VERTIGO

Yukito Ayatsuji

The Decagon House Murders
The Mill House Murders
The Labyrinth House Murders
The Clock House Murders

Boileau-Narcejac

Vertigo
She Who Was No More

Frédéric Dard

Bird in a Cage
The Wicked Go to Hell
Crush
The Executioner Weeps
The King of Fools
The Gravediggers' Bread

Friedrich Dürrenmatt

The Pledge
The Execution of Justice
Suspicion
The Judge and His Hangman

Margaret Millar

Vanish in an Instant
A Stranger in My Grave
The Listening Walls

Baroness Orczy

The Old Man in the Corner
The Case of Miss Elliott
Unravelled Knots

Edgar Allan Poe

The Paris Mysteries

Soji Shimada

The Tokyo Zodiac Murders
Murder in the Crooked House

Akimitsu Takagi

The Tattoo Murder

Josephine Tey

The Daughter of Time
The Man in the Queue

Masako Togawa

The Master Key
The Lady Killer

S. S. Van Dine

The Bishop Murder Case

Futaro Yamada

The Meiji Guillotine Murders

Seishi Yokomizo

The Honjin Murders
The Inugami Curse
The Village of Eight Graves
Death on Gokumon Island
The Devil's Flute Murders
The Little Sparrow Murders
Murder at the Black Cat Cafe
She Walks at Night